WESTERN

**KIL
CO**

WITHDRAWI

GAYLORD M

*Also by Jackson Cole
in Large Print:*

The Death Riders
The Devil's Legion
Texas Fury
Thunder Range

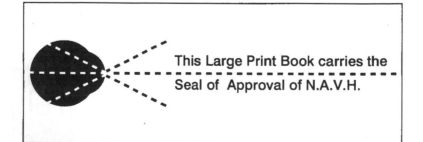

This Large Print Book carries the
Seal of Approval of N.A.V.H.

KILLER COUNTRY

Jackson Cole

G.K. Hall & Co. • Thorndike, Maine

Published in 1999 by arrangement with Golden West Literary Agency.

G.K. Hall Large Print Paperback Series.

The text of this Large Print edition is unabridged.
Other aspects of the book may vary from the original edition.

Set in 16 pt. Plantin.

Printed in the United States on permanent paper.

Library of Congress Cataloging-in-Publication Data

Cole, Jackson.
    Killer country / Jackson Cole.
       p.   cm.
    ISBN 0-7838-8719-1 (lg. print : sc : alk. paper)
    1. Large type books.   I. Title.
  [PS3505.O2685K55   1999]
  813'.54—dc21   99-35749

KILLER
COUNTRY

Doreto, the *peon,* crouched beside the window of his *adobe* hut and stared into the night. From the hut's site, a little swell of land, he could see the shifting starshine of the river, could hear its monotonous sob and murmur. The smell of the hurrying flood water of the Rio Grande was wafted to him on the wings of a lonesome little wind that wandered around the thatched *'dobe* for a moment before tramping on its weary way across the desert toward the grim battlements of the Quitmans and Cerro Blanca. That wind, slanting out of the southwest, was silent save for the endless plaint of the river. Doreto strained his ears to catch a sound he feared and dreaded and expected. Abruptly his scrawny form stiffened and a murmured *"Madre de Dios!"* slipped past his suddenly dry lips. The hurrying fingers of the wind had plucked up a sound other than that of the tireless river.

Faint it was, a silver-shod tapping sifting tremulously through the starlight, but it brought the sweat out on the *peon's* thin cheeks and widened his dark eyes. He crouched lower beside the window, peering fearfully into the shadows, the palms of his hands moist and sticky.

On came the sound, a swelling beat that grew and grew — the quick, staccato drum of a horse's fleet hoofs on the hard soil of the river bank. It came, Doreto knew, from the direction of the ford across the Rio Grande.

Up the little knoll, zigzagging along the trail worn deep by many passages of bare feet, came the horseman, looming gigantic in the dim light. There was a final clash of hoofs, a breathless pause, then the crash of a heavy quirt handle against the closed door. With trembling hands the *peon* unbarred it, swung it open, and stood, head humbly bowed, at the threshold.

The horseman leaned forward in his saddle, hissed words in a harsh voice, peremptory words that brooked no argument. Doreto quivered his thin shoulders submissively, mumbled thick acquiescence:

"*Si*, I come."

The horseman wheeled his mount, drummed down the tortuous trail and vanished into the shadows, the fading tip-tap of swift hoofs shattering the silence for a numb moment or two and then dying into nothingness. Doreto turned to face his wife who was staring at him with wide, fearful eyes from the gloom.

"You will not go, Doreto?"

"Not go! *Sangre de Cristo!* Not go when *The Rider* brings the summons! Think you of Miguel of the Ford who did not go — crucified to the spines of a chola cactus! Of Sebastian — bound to an ant hill, with the sun of noon pouring down into eyes from which the lids had been cut away! I fear to go, *si!* But I fear more to remain!"

Still muttering, he fumbled among the cords of his bed and drew from beneath the husk mattress a long-barrelled rifle. A moment later he vanished through the black opening of the door, in his ears the terrified sobbing of his wife.

Down the hill he hurried, turned west along the river bank and stumbled on through the gloom. And as he went, a wall of inky cloud climbed up the long slant of the western sky, blotting out the stars and pressing a blanket of shadows down upon the ghostly gray surface of the river. Overhead thunder muttered; there was an occasional flicker of lightning. Then on the wings of the moaning wind came the rain, level lances of icy water that beat and lashed the thin figure staggering on in the intermittent glare of the lightning. The thunder mutter grew to a crashing roar.

Through the desolation of wind and rain rode a man — a tall man mounted on a magnificent golden sorrel whose sleek coat streamed with water. The man cursed the rain in a half-humorous, half-weary voice while the sorrel snorted his unqualified disgust.

"Feller, we may be going someplace, but we sure aren't getting there, not so you can notice," the man said, blinking the water from his level green eyes.

The cayuse said something in hoss language that obviously would not bear repeating. The man chuckled, his strongly moulded, slightly wide mouth quirking up at the corners, his green eyes sunny. He swayed in the saddle with the lithe grace of one who has spent a lifetime there, his broad shoulders shrugging under the streaming slicker whose clumsy folds could not altogether conceal the lines of deep chest, slim waist and muscular thighs. His hair that showed beneath the brim of his wide hat was black as the storm clouds overhead and seemed to shed the rain without gathering any appreciable dampness. Sill chuckling to himself, he rode westward into the teeth of the storm.

Out of the darkness ahead came a staccato tapping that swiftly grew to a drumming thud. Jim Hatfield's sorrel straightened, his eyes questioning.

"Somebody seems to be in a hurry," Hatfield murmured. "Maybe he's scared he'll get wet. Guess we'd better give him room to pass."

He reined the big horse out of the trail and nearer to the sloping bank of the river. Slouching comfortably in the saddle he waited while the thud of the swift hoofs grew louder and louder.

In a blaze of golden flame the "roses of the storm" suddenly bloomed across the heavens, making the streaming landscape bright as day. Hatfield had a quick vision of a dark, sinister face rushing toward him out of the night. That and the lightning flicker of a sinewy hand.

Crash! Crash! Crash!

Hatfield was sideways out of the saddle a flickering breath before death blazed at him out of the dark. He heard the bullets yell through the space his body had occupied the instant before. Only his astounding coordination of mind and muscle had saved him.

As he left the saddle his right hand closed on the butt of the heavy rifle snugged in the saddle boot. In that one bewildering ripple of lithe movement he whirled on firm feet and flung the rifle to his shoulder. Long lances of flame spurted from the black muzzle as he raked the darkness with lead. He paused for an instant, finger curled on the trigger. Out of the night came the retreating drum of the racing horse. Again he fired, three swift shots, center, right and left.

The lightning flared again, revealing a speeding figure bending low over the neck of a horse. Hatfield's eyes glinted back of the rifle sights, but even as he pressed trigger, man and horse lurched sideways into the solid blackness of a grove that grew beside the trail. The darkness rushed down as the lightning died. The roll of the thunder drowned all other sounds.

Hatfield hesitated a second, then fumbled cartridges from his saddlebags and reloaded the rifle.

"No sense in chasing after that galoot," he told the sorrel. "Chances are, Goldy hoss, you could run him down, all right, if we managed to hit onto his trail, but chances are, too, that we'd hunt half the night before we picked it up. He's heading in the wrong direction for us, anyhow. Funny thing to do, throw down on a stranger that

11

way. Looks like he's got something on his mind. Maybe we just scared him, though. 'Pears folks get scared easy in this section, according to what we heard about it. Not much wonder, though, when you recollect what happened over here of late. Well, everything considered, I guess we'd best be ambling along toward where that town of Cuevas and *Don* Fernando Cartina's F Bar C ranch is supposed to be. June along, jughead, it's a hungry night, and sort of dampish!"

2

The storm brawled on across the sky and in its wake the wind, now chuckling happily, scoured the sky clean with final wisps of cloud. The stars, newly rinsed and burnished, blazed out again, but only for a little while. Soon they paled from gold to silver, grew white and wan, shrunk to mere pinpoints of light and winked out. As the retreating storm vanished beyond the eastern horizon, the sky flushed delicate rose, deepened to soft pink barred with gold. Bands of scarlet climbed up from the edge of the world, merged in a bewildering crimson flame shot with saffron arrows. The desert shimmered like polished bronze. The western mountains veiled themselves in exquisite purple. A bird sang. The grasses rippled blue and indigo. The sun came forth like a bridegroom from his chamber, and it was day.

Jim Hatfield rode through the winy gold of morning as he had ridden through the rain lashed blackness of the night. The sun quickly dried his sodden clothes and the glossy coat of the big sorrel. Beside a little trickle of clear water he dismounted, turned the horse loose to graze and cooked his breakfast with swift efficiency. Hot coffee, bacon, dough cake fried in the grease — he downed them all with the lusty appetite of youth and perfect health. Then, while the golden horse still cropped steadily, he stretched out in the shade of a thicket and slept like a child. Two hours later he sat up thoroughly awake, grinned at the sun and lithely got to his feet.

The stream formed a shady pool beside the thicket and Hatfield stripped and plunged in, dousing his long, lean body in the refreshing water. As he moved, the muscles rippled along sinewy back and shoulders like smooth snakes under a skin that had the sheen of satin. Flexing his long arms, he stepped from the pool and stopped dead still.

Three men had ridden up, the slight sound of their horses' unshod hoofs on the grass-grown bank drowned by the prattle of the stream. Silent and motionless they sat and stared at the tall, naked Ranger. Double cartridge belts crossed their chests. They carried rifles. A heavy revolver and a long knife sagged at the waist belt of each. They were dark of face, beady of eye, with high cheekbones and lank black hair. Almost pure-blood Yaqui Indians, Hatfield instantly perceived.

"*Buenas dias,*" he nodded, his voice mild and drawling. Silence greeted his "good day." The beady eyes remained inscrutable. Hatfield swept the dark faces with his level green gaze, apparently only mildly interested, but thinking furiously.

He was totally unarmed, his gun belt half a dozen yards distant. The sinister trio had noted the fact as he gathered from the quick furtive glances they cast in the direction of his discarded garments. To all appearances he was utterly at their mercy, and it did not need a second glance to tell him that these were men to whom the very meaning of the word was unknown. One of them spoke, his voice the harsh growl of a beast of prey —

"What do you here, *Señor?*"

"Right now," Hatfield told him, "I was taking a bath. I'm just passing through."

The other's face did not change. "We want no *gringos* here," he said with cold finality.

"I'm not staying," Hatfield replied.

The other's upper lip lifted in what was intended for a smile, showing sharply pointed white teeth — a smile of sinister menace.

"*Señor,*" he said softly, "you make the mistake. You *are* staying here!"

At the words his companions slightly shifted their rifles and a dark glitter, like the glint of bloody dagger points in the sun, appeared in their beady eyes.

The meaning of both words and gesture was unmistakable. Jim Hatfield realized it and knew he was in a desperate position. It was not the first time the man whom a grim old Lieutenant of Rangers had named "The Lone Wolf" had found himself facing desperate odds. In the course of his career as a Ranger, death had missed him more than once by the thickness of a shadow on a gray day. Some of his fellow Rangers vowed that he possessed a charmed life. What he *did* possess were nerves and muscles that obeyed instantly and without fumbling the swift, conclusive orders of a hairtrigger mind. Working alone, as was his custom, he could seldom look for assistance of any kind. His facile mind, his steely muscles and lightning-fast hands were what he depended upon, and the knowledge that they were all he *could* depend upon made him doubly dangerous to men who thought they had him at a disadvantage. In addition to these, however, there was one "friend" usually within call upon whom he could depend to the utmost of that friend's limited capabilities. He could see that friend now lifting an inquiring golden head over a clump of bush. He saw also the ripple of muscle along the half-breed leader's jaw as he made up his mind to act. That and the tensing of the dark hands that held the rifle.

Still standing unclothed and unarmed, the Ranger threw back his head and pursed his lips. A whistle-note, shrill and piercing, thrilled through the sultry air. Swift on its heels came the Lone Wolf's deep-toned shout —

"Get 'em, Goldy-hoss! At 'em, boy!"

Instantly there was a prodigious crashing of iron hoofs and a scream of rage. Down upon the startled half-breeds stormed the great golden horse, pawing, slashing, biting. One of the wiry little mustangs was bowled over like a rabbit, his rider with him. A second man shrieked in agony as the sorrel's gleaming teeth tore a great piece of flesh from his arm. They tried to shoot the tall horse, but his movements were so lightning fast and his attack so vicious they could not draw a

16

bead on him. In a split second of time they had other things to think about.

Jim Hatfield covered the distance to his gun belt like a bronze streak in the sunshine. As he yanked the heavy Colts from their sheaths, the dark-browed leader of the Mexicans sent a rifle bullet whistling over his shoulder. A second clipped a lock of dark hair from his head. Then his guns let go with a rippling crash.

The dark leader died in his saddle with two bullets laced through his heart. As he toppled to the ground, Hatfield shot the unhorsed man between the eyes as the other tried to pull trigger. He flung up his guns as the third man, blood pouring from his slashed arm, went crashing through the growth on his maddened horse. By the time Hatfield got around the thicket he was out of range, slumped low in his saddle, apparently in a faint. Hatfield watched him until he was small in the distance, reeling drunkenly but still clinging to his flying mustang. The Ranger shrugged and went back for his clothes.

"Calc'late he won't be good for much of anything except to yowl for quite a spell," he growled. "Well, horse, you sure did yourself proud. I'll remember it the next time you try to kick me loose from my pants or bite my ear off. Yes, you're quite a cayuse, even if you are so poison-mean a rattlesnake'd swell up and bust if he fanged you."

He rubbed the velvety muzzle affectionately and ducked as the bronk reached for his ear.

Then he whirled, guns stabbing out, as a voice spoke from the growth behind him —

"*Madre de Dios! Señor,* you are not long for this world!"

Over the muzzles of his ready guns Hatfield eyed the speaker, a wizened old Mexican who was staring fearfully at the sprawled bodies on the grass. He raised frightened eyes to the half-clothed Ranger and shook his grizzled head.

"Two dead!" he mumbled thickly. "Two *Riders!* And one who escaped to tell the tale!"

"Tell it to who, *amigo?*" Jim asked, sheathing his guns and smiling at the old *peon.*

The other wet his dry lips with a quivering tongue. "Assuredly," he mumbled, "assuredly will he tell *El Hombre!*"

"The Man?" Jim translated wonderingly. "What man?"

"*El Hombre* is *El Hombre,*" replied the *peon.* "None may say more than that. None may *know* more than that."

"You going to tell him, too?" Hatfield asked quietly. The other let out a choked-chicken squawk and his few teeth chattered.

"*Señor!*" he gasped, "I saw nothing! I but rested here in the shade! I know nothing! *I* speak to *El Hombre!* God forbid, or that he speak to me!"

His fear contorted face vanished and Hatfield heard him running swiftly through the growth. The Ranger finished dressing thoughtfully, the concentration furrow creased deep between his level black brows.

"Funny business," he mused. " 'Riders!' and *El Hombre*. Mexicans usually mean a lot more than just 'The Man' when they use words like that. About like when we say 'Big Boss'. Hmmm! So *El Hombre* has jiggers riding for him who don't want *gringos* around here. Evidently *The Man* doesn't want them — they're just following orders. That hard riding gent I met last night in the rain felt that way, too, evidently. And it all ties up with what Cap McDowell told me about the trouble over here. Those three hellions — the one last night, too — look like the sort of skunks who would peg poor devils over ant hills and cut off their eyelids or hang them up on chola cactuses. I should have held that old jigger who just scooted off and found out if he knew anything, only he was too scared to be of any use. I know the kind — scare 'em and all they do is lie a blue streak. Well, reckon the best thing is to keep right on riding along till we hit Cuevas. I expect that's our best bet to get the lowdown on things."

After a careful search of the dead men's clothing revealed nothing that shed any light on the mystery, Hatfield saddled Goldy and rode east once more. Overhead, outlined against the clear blue of the sky, an ominous shape sailed slowly on planing wings. Another joined it, then another. Lower and lower they glided, wrinkled, featherless necks outstretched, beady, dispassionate eyes staring coldly — Death's winged ambassadors. For the briefest flicker of an instant the dark shadow of one rested on the Ranger's face!

3

Jim Hatfield could always tell when Captain McDowell was perturbed about something. When he entered the office and saw Captain Bill aimlessly pulling papers about on his desk he nodded, draped his long body comfortably in a chair, rolled a cigarette and waited.

In the blue haze of the cigarette smoke, he pictured the first time he had sat in the office of the famous Captain of the Texas Rangers. He saw himself, younger by quite a few years, and just graduated from a famous college of engineering, tight-lipped, cold-eyed, listening to the old Ranger's quiet voice.

"Taking the law in your own hands is a bad business, Jim," said Captain Bill. "I know how you feel with your dad murdered by wideloopers and his herd run off. I know you aim to run down his killers and finish them off. But, Jim, the vengeance trail is a tricky trail to ride. Many an honest man who started riding it has ended up on the wrong side of the law, one with the hellions he set out to run down. You wouldn't want to end up like John Ringo or Doc Holliday. Both were honest men when they started out. They ended up bucking the law."

"Yes," Hatfield admitted, "but I don't intend to let those buzzards get away with it."

"You don't need to," said Captain McDowell. "But there's more ways of killing a cat than choking it to death on milk. There's a wrong way to do a thing and a right way. I'm going to give you the chance to do it the right way. I'm offering you a job with the Rangers. Then you'll be on the side of the law and you'll have all the power and prestige of the State of Texas behind you. Your first chore will be to run down those hellions. Of course," he added cannily, "after you finish it, you can always resign from the force and go back to engineering."

Hatfield heard himself, after a moment's reflection, voicing the cow country's laconic acceptance of a job —

"Well, suh, looks like you've hired yourself a hand."

Jim Hatfield brought his father's killers to justice; the chase was long and arduous, and before it was over he knew he had found his life work. It might be a short life — the chances were good that it would be — but come what may, he was a Ranger.

And now the Lone Wolf was a legend throughout the Southwest, honored and admired by honest men, hated and feared by the outlaw brand.

The picture faded. Hatfield came back to the present as Captain Bill raised his grizzled head and fixed his cold blue eyes on his Lieutenant and ace-man.

"Merry blue-blazin' hell has busted loose over

21

in the Cuevas Valley country," said Captain Bill. "Everybody is scairt bald-headed. Murders, robberies, wideloopings."

"Sounds sort of routine for that section," Hatfield commented.

"Well, it isn't," Captain Bill replied. "If that was all, I'd be inclined to agree with you. But when it gets to be common to find poor devils pegged over ant hills with their eyelids cut off, or crucified on chola cactuses, or with their tongues cut out, it's sort of out of the ordinary."

Hatfield stared, his jaw tightening.

"Yes, that's right," resumed McDowell. "A dozen or more killings of that kind have occurred there recently. And," he added impressively, "all Texas-Mexicans."

"From the northern river villages?"

"Yes. And not unnaturally, the villages are in somewhat of a turmoil. You know what that can mean."

Hatfield looked grave, but said nothing.

"So far as I can gather," said Captain Bill, "somebody has deliberately set out to terrorize the villages — and for no good end."

Hatfield nodded his understanding. "Juan Flores and Cheno Cartinas, among others, used that method to get control of the villages north and south of the Rio Grande. And the Border ran red in consequence. Cartinas and his bunch actually captured Brownsville and occupied the city of three thousand people for some little time."

"That's right," agreed Captain Bill. "Funny, you mentioning Cheno Cartinas. In the letter I just got from Sheriff Raines of Cuevas county he mentions a jigger by the name of Cartina who seems to be considerable of a feller in that section. Spanish descent. Owns mines and a big ranch. Appears to have considerable influence with the villagers. Raines speaks well of him, but he might be worth keeping an eye on. Never can tell about that sort. They usually hold to the traditions of the old *Dons* and sometimes go on the prod, especially if they think they've been done an injustice. Long on blood feuds south of the Rio Grande, and their evening-up methods usually aren't nice."

Hatfield chuckled. "Cartina!" he repeated. "And south of the Rio Grande, over around that section, is a bandit leader called Cheno — Cheno the Merciless. He's raised plenty of hell and shoved a chunk under a corner. Has even got old President Diaz buffaloed, or so folks say. Keeps a standing army of his own, has his own town, and just about runs things to suit himself which doesn't suit a lot of other folks. Never raided this side of the Line, though, so far as I've heard."

"Well, if you can go on what Raines says, he's raiding this side now," Captain Bill grunted. "But Raines is liable to be prejudiced. He's an old-time Border peace officer and his kind usually are down on Mexicans, even if they are American citizens of two or three generations on this side of the Line. If they happen to have a few

23

drops of Spanish blood they're all Mexicans to those old jiggers."

Hatfield nodded his understanding. "They're good people if let alone," he said. "But they're easily led and easy to stir up, and when they do get on the prod they can be *muy malo*."

"Uh-huh, plenty bad," Captain Bill agreed soberly.

"Raines mention anybody else over there?" Hatfield asked.

"Uh-huh," said Captain Bill. "Several ranchers who have been losing stock, feller by the name of Preston, for one. Raines doesn't 'pear to think over much of him, but says he's entitled to protection same as anybody else, even though he is a wild sort and is looked at sideways by some folks. He also mentions a feller named Garrett who, it seems, is in jail somewhere down in Mexico. Went down there with Preston and some others to try to get back stock he figured Cheno rustled: Preston was the only one who got back alive. Raines says Garrett's spread is about the best in the section. Says Cartina owns a good one, too, but his chief interest is mines and he's lost several valuable gold shipments. Oh, some hellion is feathering his nest for fair. But here's the letter. You can read it when you get time. One name in it don't pass over — Ab Carlysle. The outlaw bunch raided the Cuevas bank of which Carlysle was president. Ab fought 'em off with a shotgun and a couple of sixes. Killed a couple. I used to work with Carlysle in the old

24

days, Rocking Chair spread. I liked him." The captain's lined face was suddenly bleak.

Hatfield glanced inquiringly at his chief.

"They found Ab in an alley two nights later," said Captain Bill. "Throat was cut from ear to ear and other things were done to him. Raines doesn't say just what, but it must have been pretty bad."

Hatfield said nothing, but his strangely colored eyes turned the shade of snow-dusted ice on a bitter winter morning.

"So Jed Raines, a salty proposition, is yelling for help," Captain Bill summed up. "Wants a troop sent down. And you know I've got no troop to spare right now. So —"

Hatfield grinned and stood up. "So I guess I'd better ride down that way for a look-see," he remarked.

"Good notion," said Captain Bill. "If you need help, let out a squawk and I'll see what I can do for you."

"Uh-huh, I'll do that," the Lone Wolf replied cheerfully as he passed out the door.

"Uh-huh, like the devil you will!" chuckled Captain Bill as the door closed on the Ranger's broad back. "When *you* yelp for help, me, I'm going to fork me the fastest hoss what's handy and hightail — in the other direction, 'cause right then I calculate the only person that can do anybody any good is God Almighty himself!"

Hatfield was running over the contents of the

letter in his mind as he rode out of the red eye of the sunset. He had destroyed the missive, but his practiced memory retained its most minute details. Right now he was checking the directions they gave for reaching Cuevas.

"Guess that sawtooth mountain ahead is the one that Raines said is right back of the town," he mused, squinting at the lofty peak about whose massive shoulders the approaching dusk was drawing a robe of royal purple. "Letter said Cuevas was built at the foot of a spur that runs down almost to the Rio Grande. Guess those hills, that sort of make easy stepping up to the mountain, are where the mines are. Mighty fine looking range land between here and the hills. Funny thing, stretch of range like this set down almost in the middle of the desert. This whole section is what's left of a high plain that was worn down more by wind and sun beating on a bare surface than by rain. That's what accounts for the queer looking battlements and mesas and faults and escarpments — they're just surviving fragments of that old plain whose level was once above the tops of the highest of them. And now us big-feeling jiggers come crawling around the foot of those old spires that have been looking down on things hereabouts for more millions of years than even the geologists can agree on. Guess we aren't such-a-much after all, Goldy."

The sun sank lower, the light rays leveled out and tinged the blue wind-ripples of the prairie grass with flame. Hatfield could make out a faint smudge rising against the eastern sky. He knew it to be the smoke from the smelters and stamp mills of Cuevas, the raw, turbulent gold strike town clinging to the gray flanks of the hills.

"Got another hour or so of daylight," he calculated, squinting at the low lying sun. "Boss, I figure we might as well eat before trying to make it to town. Things look closer in this air than they really are — quite a step over to that ridge. I've got enough chuck left for another helping. And as for you, you old grass burner, all you got to do is drop your nose down and help yourself to a square meal any time you take a notion. Get going, jughead, we'll head for that creek over to the left. Right now my stomach's so empty she's slid clean in behind my backbone!"

The creek, a shallow trickle of clear water with sedgy banks, was bordered by a moderately wide belt of thick growth. Hatfield headed for a little clearing that opened out onto the prairie across which he was riding. On the far side of the stream the clearing was walled in by thick bristles of chaparral. It sloped gently to the water's edge.

The sorrel was thirsty. "All right," Hatfield told him, "go ahead and drink while I get a fire started. Then I'll slip the rig off and you can take a roll; we're not staying here long."

With the efficiency of the old campaigner, the Ranger had a clear blaze going in a very few minutes. He carefully stacked more dry wood on it, desiring a bed of glowing coals over which cooking could be done with a minimum of smoke and resulting profanity. He was turning to care for the horse when a muffled querulous bawl sounded from a little distance down the stream. He glanced that way, noted the deeper green of the swamp land, and listened for a repetition of the bawl.

It came again, undoubtedly from a weary and struggling throat. Jim had heard that kind of a bellow before, time without number. Instead of uncinching the sorrel he swung into the saddle and loosened his rope.

"Darn calf got himself bogged down in the mud," he remarked to Goldy. "We got to snake him out before he drowns or the coyotes do for him."

He skirted a clump of growth, shoved the sorrel through another and saw the calf. The animal, almost half grown, was firmly held in the sticky swamp mud. Already it had sunk to its knees. Soon it would be completely engulfed. Hatfield measured the distance with his eye and flipped a lazy loop toward the straining head. The noose settled about the calf's neck and he tightened it with an easy pull so as not to strangle the dogie. Then he sent Goldy slowly up the bank, dragging the choking, squawk-bellerin' creature out of the mud. Once it was in the clear he eased off the pressure and the calf floundered up the bank. It limped badly, however, and he could see a smear of blood on one haunch.

"Guess we'd better haul you over to the fire and take a look at that leg," he decided.

The calf didn't particularly want to go, but it didn't have much choice in the matter. In the clearing, a quick flip of the rope and the creature went down. Hatfield dismounted, leaving Goldy to keep the rope taut, and bent over the calf which lay bawling beside the fire.

"Not broken," he nodded, feeling of the injured limb; "just a bad cut. I'll put a little liniment on it and you'll be okay." He straightened up to get the bottle from his saddlebags.

Wham!

Hatfield nearly turned a backward flipflop as a bullet knocked his fire to smoking fragments. He felt the wind of it and felt a little more than the wind of a second that followed close on its heels. This one knocked a bit of skin from the back of his left hand. Before the third got there — and it got there fast — he was hidden in the growth, swearing softly to himself and peering across the stream. A fourth slug showered him with leaves and twigs; but it did tip off the approximate position of the gunman. Silently as a wraith of drifting smoke he faded through the growth, working swiftly upstream to where the creek was narrow and rock strewn. He slipped around a bend and flitted across the stream, using the rocks for stepping stones. In the growth on the far bank he redoubled his caution as he glided back downstream. He diagonalled away from the water until he was directly opposite the clearing. Moving with the smooth grace of a hunting mountain lion, he approached the final fringe of thicket.

4

Roaring Bill McDowell had once visioned Jim Hatfield as a mountain lion poised on a lonely crag in the moonlight, ready to dare the black depths beneath in one tremendous, death-defying leap. Could the old Ranger Captain have seen him at the moment, he would have been more than ever struck by the aptness of his simile. The Lone Wolf's long, lithe body was tensely crouched, his leg muscles propelling him like powerful snakes. He had sensed rather than seen the slightest hint of movement at the base of a bush-shadowed boulder a little ways down the sloping bank. An instant later he leaped as the panther leaps, steely fingers outstretched. He landed beside the solid shadow huddled behind the boulder and peering across the stream.

"Gotcha!" he growled exultantly. In another instant his arms were filled with wildcat fighting fury. He gave a gasp of amazement and tightened his grip on the slim figure of a small red-haired girl whose big blue eyes blazed into his and whose breath panted between her red lips. Before he knew it there was a long scratch down his left cheek and a couple more on his neck. White little teeth fastened on the back of his hand. A sun-golden little fist beat a tattoo on his broad breast.

"Hold it, Ma'am!" he bawled "I'm not going to hurt you. I'll turn you loose if you promise to be good!"

For answer she kicked his shins with small riding boots and tried to bite him a second time. Jim shook her till her teeth rattled and she gasped for breath.

"Listen, you little hellion," he grated, "if you don't behave I'm going to turn you over my knee and spank you till you'll eat standing up for a week! What's the matter with you, anyhow? Gone plumb *loco?*"

Suddenly he felt the little body go limp in his grasp. An instant later she broke into convulsive sobbing.

"I — I know you're going to kill me!" she gasped.

With effortless ease Jim picked her up, plucked her fallen rifle from beside the boulder with one hand and strode with her out into the open. There he set her on her feet and regarded her in the last light of the dying day. His green eyes were sunny and his wide mouth was grin-quirked at the corners. The girl stared at him, fear struggling with surprise. As he continued to smile down at her from his great height the fear vanished altogether and the surprise deepened.

"Why — why you can't be *working* for the Preston outfit!" she exclaimed.

"Preston outfit?" Jim repeated questioningly.

"Yes," said the girl, "Brant Preston's Circle P."

"Nope, I don't work for the Circle P," Jim told

31

her. "What made you think I did?"

"Because," replied the girl angrily, "Brant Preston hires all the gunmen and rustlers that drift in here."

Her blue eyes flashed as she glanced across the stream to where Goldy, obedient to orders, still held the rope taut on the protesting dogie.

"Even if you don't work for Brant Preston, I'd like to have you explain about altering the brand on my calf!" she exclaimed.

"Altering the brand on your calf!" Jim wondered. "Why Ma'am, I wasn't doing a job of slick ironing."

"What were you dragging it up to your fire for then?" she demanded. "I watched you throw it and hogtie it. Why did you do that if you weren't going to blot the brand?"

Jim chuckled, his green eyes sunnier than ever. "Come on, *Señorita*," he said, leading the way toward where he had crossed the stream, "the best thing I can do is show you what I was doing; that'll explain things better than talking about it."

When they reached the rocky narrows he picked her up lightly again and carried her across; she offered no objection, not even when he continued to carry her until they reached the clearing. The hogtied calf gave a final weary and querulous bawl as they approached. Hatfield gestured to its gashed haunch and to the mud with which it was smeared. As the girl examined the injured animal with little exclamations of pity, he procured the liniment bottle from his saddlebags and gave the wound a liberal application. The calf bawled to high heaven as the fiery medicine soaked into the open wound, but when Hatfield eased off the rope it scrambled to its feet and limped off with many an indignant backward glance.

"He'll make out now," chuckled the Ranger. "Sore as Hades, inside and out, but nothing he won't get over."

He replaced the liniment bottle and slipped the rig off Goldy.

"Got time to eat with me?" he asked. "I want to make it to town tonight and I figured there was no sense in taking that ride on an empty stomach."

The girl hesitated. "I really should be heading back to the ranch," she said, "but I guess things can get along without me for a while."

She paused and then looked the tall Ranger full in the eyes. "First thing, I wish to apologize for misjudging you," she said. "We have lost so much stock of late that I was furious when I saw what appeared to be another steal going on right before my eyes. I'm sorry I knocked dust in your eyes."

"You came darn near doing more than knock it in my eyes. If you could just shoot a bit straighter, you'd likely have dusted both sides of my coat."

The girl glanced at him, a ghost of a smile touching her red lips. She picked up the light rifle and her eyes travelled over the clearing.

To the west, across the stream and quite a distance away, was a tall blasted pine. On the topmost dead branch, upon an almost vertical spire of rotting wood, perched an old hawk, his gray shape outlined sharply against the red of the evening sky. Shadows were already thick in the clearing and the light was dim and uncertain.

"Watch the hawk," she said, lifting the rifle.

"Hold on," exclaimed Hatfield, "Not that feller — those gray-legs are good citizens, eat nothing but bugs and such."

"Oh, I won't hurt him," she replied, steadying the rifle. "Watch me knock his perch out from under him."

The next instant the amazed hawk was hurtling upward, squawking his indignation. The rotten branch on which he roosted was spattering down through the tree and the echoes of the waspish rifle crack were blundering about among the trunks.

Jim nodded gravely to the smiling girl.

"Thank you, Ma'am," he said, "for shooting at the fire."

5

Darkness had fallen by the time they finished the meal, but before the earth had really got the feel of the soft blanket of shadows spread by the dying fingers of the day, a round yellow moon soared up over the edge of the world and drenched desert and rangeland with a flood of silver rain. It was so light that each mesquite thorn stood out clear and bold like a tiny spear in the hands of elfin warriors. The girl and the man rode the white blaze of the trail with the shimmer of the moonlight before them and their shadows stretching long and black behind. They rode silently for some time, held by the spell of beauty the moonfire wove over hill and mesa and rolling range. Their horses' irons rang loud on the hard trail, the rippling echoes setting the coyotes to yipping and causing a venerable and hungry owl to bawl in protest at the untimely interruption of his hunting.

"My name is Lonnie Garrett," the girl told him. "I own the Bowtie spread — this is my range we're on now. Yes, I run it by myself. My mother died when I was born and last year my father rode into Mexico — and didn't ride back."

"Killed down there?"

"Worse," she replied, her lips tight with pain. "He and Brant Preston and another rancher,

Craig Doyle, who owned the K8, rode into Mexico to get back some steers that were rustled from this side. They had three or four cowboys with them. Doyle and the cowboys were killed. Dad and Brant Preston were taken prisoner. Preston managed to escape from jail, but he left Dad behind. He's still there. We've tried to get him out; but Cheno, the bandit, runs all that section of the country and nobody can do anything with Cheno. I'm afraid poor Dad will die there."

Jim nodded sympathetically and the girl changed the subject.

"East of my range," she said, "between here and Cuevas and on into the hills is *Don* Fernando Cartina's F Bar C. To the east of Cuevas is Brant Preston's Circle P. The range peters out into the desert farther east, but it's good land. The deep coulees and canyons make good shelter from heat and snow. Grass stays good and uncovered most all winter in the draws."

"Sort of a widelooper's idea of Heaven, though, if they operate in the section." Hatfield commented.

"Yes," the girl said dryly. "The man who owns such a range has his hands full with rustlers, unless they happen to be friendly."

Hatfield's dark brows lifted slightly and he shot her a swift glance which she did not appear to notice.

"The Cingaro Trail runs across the Circle P." she commented with apparent irrelevance.

"Cingaro Trail?" Jim repeated.

"Yes, the trail the smugglers and rustlers and robbers use to cross into Mexico. It runs through Pardusco Canyon. Only the outlaws can follow it. In Pardusco Canyon it branches many times and the branches run through side canyons and gorges and wind and twist until one who is unfamiliar with their windings is hopelessly lost. That is why it is so easy to run stock in this section and why stage robbers and murderers find so little difficulty in losing the sheriff when he rides after them. It is a terrible place, Pardusco Canyon; it is white with bones."

"The Gypsy Trail and Grizzly Canyon," Hatfield translated; "sounds interesting. Does the trail run anywhere near Cuevas?"

"Yes," Lonnie told him. "After passing across the Circle P range it slants west across *Don* Fernando's F Bar C and enters the canyon. The canyon runs almost due west for quite a way and passes Cuevas about five miles to the north. There is said to be a trail out of Cuevas that enters the canyon; but if there is, nobody but the outlaws know it."

"The Cingaro Trail crosses your spread, too?" Hatfield asked.

"No," the girl said, "it continues north to New Mexico."

"I see," Jim nodded.

"*Don* Fernando is a fine man," the girl added earnestly. "Old Spanish stock and a perfect gentleman. He is always doing things for the poorer

37

people and he pays his riders and his workers in the mine the best of wages and is very kind to them. He has only Mexicans riding for him, except for Pierce Kimble, his foreman, but he employs Americans as well as Mexicans in his mine. You'll like *Don* Fernando, if you should meet him."

Hatfield was destined to meet *Don* Fernando, and soon.

For a mile or more they rode in silence. Jim was busy with his thoughts.

"That Brant Preston gent'll bear some 'vestigatin', it looks like," he mused. "The Cingaro business sounds interesting, too. Wide-looping and drygulching gents have to go somewhere. If you can manage to cut across the road they travel, it isn't hard to tangle their rope."

He ran swiftly over what the girl had told him relative to the position of the various ranches and the town of Cuevas. From that information he constructed a map of the region in his mind. It corresponded very well with what he had learned during his talk with Captain McDowell. The territory formed roughly a right triangle, the hypotenuse of which was the irregular line of the silvery river. The three spreads Lonnie Garrett had mentioned were snugged in the angle formed by the river and the wavering edge of the desert proper. To the north and west were other ranches, chiefly on the far side of the range of hills in the vestibule of which Cuevas was built. The big saw-tooth mountain shouldered up north of the hills and near the New Mexico line. Beyond the strip of desert on the far side of the river loomed the purple mountains of Mexico. It was a gloomily beautiful land, this vast stretch of rich range banded by strips of desert and slashed by canyon and gorge — beautiful and sinister. The Ranger, sensitive to the moods of a country as to those of men, could feel the tenseness and the threat that brooded over the moon-drenched landscape.

"No law west of the Pecos!" men had said for years. And here was the last frontier, the final stronghold of predatory forces that recognized no authority save that of their own desires. Evil things had happened recently in this dark and bloody land where the passions of diverse races clashed sharply, too many to be explained as mere sporadic outbursts of lawlessness. Jim Hatfield instinctively "knew" that he was pitted against a tight organization of some kind, probably headed by one man or a small, closely knit group that knew exactly what it wanted and was determined to get it, a band utterly indifferent as to what means were used just so long as they served. It was the kind of thing the Lone Wolf had been up against before, but never to date had he encountered evidence of such ruthlessness and callous cruelty.

"Looks like this gang, whoever they are, could teach the Comanches and Apaches things," he mused as they topped a swelling rise and saw the white ribbon and the trail tumble swiftly toward a distant dark blot that marked a spreading grove. His eyes narrowed slightly and he stared at the shadowy oblong of the growth.

"I turn north just beyond the grove," the girl remarked, following the direction of his gaze. "What are you looking at?"

"Maybe it's somebody coming to look for you," replied Hatfield. "Several somebodies."

"I don't see anything," said Lonnie staring perplexedly.

"You will soon as they ride out of the shadow," Hatfield told her. "They left the trees a minute ago."

A moment later she exclaimed sharply. "Yes, I can see them now — what eyes you have!" she wondered.

"About a dozen or so, riding fast," the Ranger commented. Instinctively his slim right hand dropped to the butt of the heavy Colt snugged against his muscular thigh and loosened it slightly in its sheath. In the same flowing motion the reins were shifted to his right hand and the left-hand gun touched lightly. So swift and casual had been the gesture that his companion did not notice. Her eyes were fixed on the tight group that rode swiftly up the trail to meet them.

On came the horsemen, riding with effortless ease, each seeming a part of the animal he bestrode. They numbered eleven with one riding somewhat in advance, a tall man who swayed in his high-pommelled Mexican saddle with lithe grace. Jim could see now that he wore the colorful garb of a *vaquero,* his *serape* sweeping across his broad breast, the moonlight glinting on silver conchas and spurs. The Ranger's keen glance also took in the rifle snugged in a saddle boot and the plain dark guns at his sinewy waist.

"May be a Mex, but he doesn't go in for pearl handles like so many of 'em do," he mused. "I need just one guess to say who he is!"

A moment later his lips twitched in a grin of satisfaction at the girl's exclamation —

"Why, it's *Don* Fernando!"

She waved her hand and gave a call; the horsemen were now less than a hundred yards distant, thundering toward the pair, crowding every inch of the trail. Goldy snorted and Hatfield instinctively tensed. Then he gave a low whistle. "That's riding!" he applauded under his breath.

Less than a score of paces away the group clashed to a halt on sliding hoofs. Perfectly motionless, horses and men, they froze like statues while the tall leader rode slowly forward. His heavy *sombrero* swept low in a salute and he bowed with courtly grace. Jim expected a precise speech in stately Spanish. He was surprised at the easy, offhand greeting —

"Hello, Miss Garrett, what are you doing out so late all by yourself?"

Don Fernando's speech was different from the careless drawl and slur of the American-Texan, but he had not a trace of accent nor the somewhat stilted choosing of words that usually marks the Spanish blood.

"I'm not alone," smiled Lonnie. "*Don* Fernando, this is Mr. Jim Hatfield who is looking for a job of riding. Mr. Hatfield, *Don* Fernando Cartina whom I was telling you about."

"You'll have to excuse me, Mr. Hatfield," said *Don* Fernando, his white teeth flashing under his small black moustache in an answering smile. "When Miss Garrett is around, I just naturally don't see anybody else."

"Can't say as I blame you, suh," agreed Jim as *Don* Fernando shook hands with a firm grip. To himself he said; "So good looking he makes your eyes bat. All steel wire and whipcord. A real *hidalgo,* or I never saw one."

"I stopped at your place," *Don* Fernando was saying to the girl. "Molly said you rode west early in the afternoon. I figured you'd ride back along the Cuevas trail and took a chance on meeting you."

He wheeled his horse as he spoke and reined in beside Lonnie. The ranks of the *vaqueros* opened as they rode forward and then closed in behind. Jim glanced across at *Don* Fernando who was chatting lightly with the girl.

Fernando Cartina was handsome, astonishingly so. Tall, lithe, broad of shoulder and trim of waist, he was little darker than the bronzed Ranger. His hair was black and inclined to curl. His eyes were large and flashing, his patrician features a cameo perfection of contour. A square jaw and firm mouth relieved his face of any hint

42

of effeminacy. He held his head high with the pride of bearing of his people. It was a powerful face and an intelligent one. His lips were very thin, but finely formed. He nodded to Hatfield in a friendly way and addressed himself to him.

"I can offer you a job in my mines, but I don't imagine it would interest you," he said. "I hire only *vaqueros* on my ranch, but I will be glad to recommend you to my friends. If you don't connect with anything, ride up to my *hacienda* and I will see what I can do."

Jim thanked *Don* Fernando and as the latter concentrated his attention on Lonnie Garrett, the Ranger dropped back a pace or two until he was riding with the silent *vaqueros*. They glanced at him obliquely from their dark eyes but said nothing.

"Mexicans with more Yaqui blood than Spanish," he decided after covertly studying them. "Plumb different brand from their boss. Top hands, no doubt about that, and mean as hungry Gila monsters if necessary. The kind the old *Dons* of Mexico keep for their private armies. Reckon *Don* Fernando is rather Mexican in his way of thinking, even though he is Texan born and his pappy and grandpappy behind him. Salty *hombres,* those old *Dons.*"

They reached the grove and rode through its dense shadows. As they reached the final fringe of growth on the far side, Hatfield's ear caught the rhythmical tapping of a swiftly ridden horse. When they rode into the moonlight once more, the tapping had grown to a steady drum. The Ranger leaned forward in his saddle and peered ahead with interest.

About six hundred yards distant another trail cut at right angles the one they were riding. It flowed out of the jumble of hills to the north and wound south, soon plunging into a scattering of buttes and chimneys beyond which, only a few miles distant, was the yellow flood of the river. Along this trail, speeding toward the intersection, came a single horseman, superbly mounted. He leaned low over his horse's neck and urged the flying animal to greater effort. Like a specter in the moonlight he came, and like a specter he vanished among the grotesque spires to the south. The swift drum died to a whisper, the whisper to blank emptiness. Only a patch of white foam, perishing in a clump of grass beside the main trail, remained as evidence that horse and rider had been real and not a figment of the imagination, born of the white moonfire and the blue shadows.

In the instant of his passing he had turned to gaze at the approaching group, and in that fleeting moment Jim Hatfield had a vision of a dark sinister face rushing toward him out of the night — just such a glimpse as had been vouchsafed him on that other night of wind and rain and roaring storm. The concentration furrow was deep between his green eyes as he relaxed in his saddle once more. Through the ranks of the *vaqueros* ran a tense whisper —

44

"El Caballero! El Caballero!"

Jim translated the exclamation, identical in meaning with that which had fallen from the stiff lips of the old *peon* as he stared at the two dead Yaquis beside the little stream —

The Rider!

6

A mile further on the trail branched. The main fork continued east, the other, a narrower and fainter track, ambled leisurely toward the north. Here the group pulled up. The girl urged Hatfield to spend the night at the Bowtie but he declined.

"I want to get an early start looking around in the morning."

"Well, this trail leads to my ranchhouse; any time you feel like visiting the Bowtie, you know how to get there," invited Lonnie.

"And anybody will tell you how to get to the F Bar C," added *Don* Fernando.

Jim thanked them both and watched them vanish up the winding trail, riding very close together, their grim silent escort a few yards behind.

"They make a pair to draw," mused the Ranger as he turned Goldy's head toward the faint glow against the sky that marked Cuevas. He grinned a little wryly and chuckled at himself. "A fine little girl," he mused; "wonder if *that's* why I can't seem to cotton to that good looking jigger she seems so interested in. Well, after all, being a Ranger doesn't keep a man from being human and she is cute as a spotted pony."

He laughed aloud and straightway forgot all about the red-haired girl, his thoughts turning to the sinister figure of the mysterious "rider" who had flashed past like some veiled phantom of the night. Ahead, lying like a leprous sore on a lovely face, appeared one of the strange bands of desert that striped the rich rangeland. Butte and chimney and wind-gnawed spire rose grotesquely from the arid surface of shifting sands. Cholla cactuses brandished their weird devil-arms in the moonlight. Greasewood with white interlaced branches and inconspicuous greenish flowers looked like the twisted skeletons of tortured ghosts. Once or twice Hatfield noted a pale glimmer which he knew to be the phosphorescent light that glowed in a skull.

Abruptly the Ranger pulled the yellow horse to a halt. Mouth suddenly dry, a moist clamminess reeking his palms, he sat and stared at the thing of blasted horror from which the moonlight seemed to shudder away.

"God!" he breathed between set teeth. "Hearing about it and *seeing* it is different!"

Gaunt, sinister, a Cholla cactus loomed large beside the trail, and crucified among the needle-sharp spines was what had once been a man. Now he was a thing to make the very coyotes and desert snakes shrink away. Broken, twisted, caked with dried blood, the motionless form still vividly portrayed the awful writhings of unthinkable agony. The face was a tortured mask that seemed to scream with silent mouth and glare with eyeless sockets to the passionless stars.

Steeling himself, the Ranger rode closer and as he peered at the pitiful remains, his eyes grew cold

47

as the gray winter sea and in their depths smoky little flames flickered like fire under ice; the man was dead but a few hours at most. Perhaps less than a full sixty minutes had passed since he screamed out his life in blood and horror.

In the Lone Wolf's brain was a beat like a soft hammer — such a sound as is made by swift hoofs speeding across desert sand. Before his eyes a vision of a sinister dark face rushing toward him out of the night flickered again.

"El Caballero!" he repeated. Lean jaw set like iron, he turned his horse's head again toward Cuevas. "Yes, they are the hellions I've got business with — those devil 'Riders'! They and that buzzard the old *peon* called *'The Man'!*"

The glow of Cuevas became a myriad twinkle and the air quivered with the steady, monotonous pound of the mining town's never-resting stamp mills. Soon the twinkles were the lighted squares of many windows and the pound of the stamps was but the undertone of the squalling roar that surged up from saloon and gambling hell and dance hall and pleasure palace where men who rode the green rangeland and men who burrowed in the depths of the lurid earth relieved hard toil with harder pleasure, gave no thought to tomorrow, looked death in the face and told him to go about his business and be damned to him!

Even as the Ranger rode slowly along the crowded main street in search of shelter and provender for his weary horse, another rider tore into town from the north, his horse's coat reeking with sweat and white with foam. Dark of face, furtive of eye, he paused before a dimly lighted *cantina* that huddled in the very shadow of the gaunt mine buildings. He left his spent bronk standing with widespread legs and hanging head and slipped through a rear door of the ramshackle saloon.

A hard faced bartender caught his glance and nodded toward a corner table beside which sat other dark men with wide *sombreros* pulled low over their eyes and glasses of fiery *tequila* in their hands. For tense moments the high crowns of the *sombreros* huddled close together, voices sounded terse gutturals. Then one by one, four lithe figures stood up from the table and vanished through the black rectangle of the door. Left behind was a single man whose arm was swathed in bandages but whose eyes glowed with an unholy light and who licked his thin lips as in pleasurable anticipation.

A newcomer sauntered across the room and dropped into one of the vacant chairs.

"You smile, Pedro," he remarked in greeting. "Your thoughts — they are pleasant?"

"*Si*," nodded the other grimly. "*Si*, I think — on revenge!"

"Ha!" The questioner's voice was understanding. He cast a significant glance at the bandaged arm —

"A knife? A bullet!"

"No," resumed the injured man. "A *horse!*"

49

7

Hatfield found a livery stable and turned Goldy over to a yawning hostler after personally seeing to it that the sorrel was properly cared for. Then he sauntered onto the main street again and looked up a restaurant.

"I hanker to surround a double portion of hog-hip-and cackle-berries," he told the bland Chinaman who waited on him.

"Can do," smiled the Chinaman. "Put up top-side fire. You like um eggs bottom side top or under?"

"Whatever you say," Hatfield sighed resign-edly. "I'm not going to get into any argument with you about it. You twirl your loop and I'll rare back and tie fast."

"Can do," agreed the Chinaman. "Cook um two times twice, bottom too."

After finishing his meal, Hatfield sat smoking and thinking about his next move. He decided to avoid Sheriff Jed Raines for the present. The Lone Wolf was averse to seeking assistance at any time. In this instance, he shrewdly deduced that he would get little of any value from the sheriff. He had read between the lines of the peace officer's letter and realized that the bluff old frontiersman was utterly unfitted to cope with such a situation as had arisen in his county.

It was a Ranger job and the Rangers had a code.

"I'll just play a lone hand for a spell," was his decision.

Pinching out his smoke he left the restaurant and strolled along the busy street. Late though the hour was, every saloon was crowded. Orchestras whined and boots thumped. Voices bawled song, other voices bawled curses. It was hard to tell which were the more unmusical. The high-pitched laughter of women cut through the deep rumble of the men.

"Wonder if they do this every night, or is it payday or something?" Hatfield asked himself. He entered a brilliantly lighted saloon, unaware that dark eyes watched him pass through the swinging doors — eyes that smouldered with hate, in the depths of which was a look of fixed purpose. He found a place at the long bar and ordered whiskey. Glass in hand he leaned against the bar and surveyed the room.

It was big and crowded with a dance floor at one end, a couple of roulette wheels and a number of poker tables all going full blast. On his high stool perched the lookout, a sawed-off shotgun across his knees, his glance flickering from table to table, alert for arguments that might become serious or a quick raid on the stacks of gold pieces resting beside the elbow of each banker. The air of the place was tolerant but reckless.

"Like open kegs of gunpowder sitting around in a hot kitchen," Hatfield decided, finishing his drink and calling for another.

Studying the groups at the various tables, his attention was attracted by a poker game that was in progress not far from the bar. Five men sat in, quiet, low spoken men who appeared intent on their game but whose eyes flickered up from their cards each time the swinging doors creaked on their hinges. The big room was well sprinkled with Mexicans in velvet and silver and gay *serapes,* but the five at the table were obviously Texans. Jim quickly noted the one who appeared to dominate the group. He was as dark of complexion as the swarthy men from below the Line. A second glance told the Ranger, however, that his eyes instead of being black were so darkly blue as to appear so and were fringed with sooty lashes. His hair was as jet as Hatfield's own. Hard of eye and hard of mouth, he was above middle height, slim and lithe.

Hatfield studied the man's dark, slightly sinister face, his own black brows drawing together. There was something familiar about it.

The swinging doors creaked and the men at the table looked up quickly. They were seated so that each member could see the doors without turning around, a fact not lost on the Ranger. He also glanced in the direction of the doors.

Four men had just entered, undoubtedly Mexicans with Yaqui blood predominating. Their *sombreros* were pulled low and their black eyes glinted in the shadow of the broad brims. In a compact group they moved across the room and lined up at the bar on Hatfield's left. They did not even glance at him as they ordered *tequila* and paid for it with a gold piece. Hatfield took no notice of them, apparently, but out of the corner of his eye he watched them in the mirror of the back bar and saw the thin lips of the man nearest to him move in an inaudible remark. The man raised his filled glass toward his lips and in doing so managed to strike it against the Ranger's shoulder. The fiery liquor splashed back into his face and spilled over his gaudy *serape*, leaving a dark stain on the blanket's bright surface. The move had all the appearance of an accident but Hatfield knew that it was intentional on the man's part, perfectly timed and calculated. With an easy grace he turned to face the other who let out a Spanish curse.

"*Caramba!* I am insult!" he bawled. "You knock the drink to my face! You look for fight!"

Like a blur of dark light his hand flashed down and up, but even as the knife gleamed, Hatfield hit him right and left and sent him crashing in a senseless heap to the floor. Instantly his companions yelled their rage and went for guns and knives. The room seemed to explode with the roar of sixshooters.

Weaving, ducking, sidestepping backwards until he was against the wall, Hatfield hammered the group with bullets. He downed one man, smashed the shoulder of a second, and shot the gun from the hand of the third. Blood streaming from a gashed cheek, holes in his hat and shirt sleeve, he crouched behind his smoking guns, green eyes sweeping the room which was in a pandemonium. Yells, curses, and the screams of women and the bellows of the lookout filled the air. The man Hatfield knocked down raised his head dazedly and glared about. Intelligence returned with a rush and he whipped out his gun. The Ranger shot him squarely between his flaming eyes. Across the room a howl of anger went up. The Mexicans there were rallying to the call of blood.

"Keel!" "Keel the *gringo!*" "*Cospital!*" "*Maldito!*" "Keel!"

Jim swept the room with a swift glance. The door was hopelessly blocked, so were the windows, all save one, a side window to his right, but there was a stretch of open floor to cover before he could hope to reach it. He noted in a glance that the group of Texans at the table were on their feet staring at him in amazement. Their hands were on their guns, but they made no move of any sort.

Guns were banging across the room, bullets whined past the Ranger.

Suddenly both his heavy Colts tipped up and fire streamed from the black muzzle. One of the big hanging lamps slammed against the ceiling. A second was blasted from its moorings and hit the floor in a shower of sparks and oil. Out went the third and last lamp and darkness blanketed the room. Hatfield slammed his guns into their holsters, went across the open floor space like a drifting shadow and through the side window in a crashing dive. Behind him sounded a terrific bedlam of yells, howls, curses and shots. He hit the thick dust of a dark alley, rolled over and came to his feet like a cat as a form thudded in the dust beside him. His Colt flashed out and the long barrel jammed into the stomach of a man as the latter staggered erect. By the shimmer of the moonlight he recognized the swarthy man who had dominated the group at the poker table.

"Don't shoot, feller," the man gasped. "We had to get out, too. There's fifty oilers in there boilin' for the kill. Here come my boys — let four out and shoot the next one."

Hatfield slewed in behind the other as dark figures shot through the smashed window.

"Come on," growled a deep bass voice. "We're all out. Come on before the locoed ol' fool of a sheriff, with his deputy, gets here and wants to lock somebody up. He'll blame us for what happened. Come on."

"You come along, too, feller," urged the dark-faced man. "Pen that hogleg and come along with us. I'll lay to it you don't hanker to be locked up, either."

Jim Hatfield's mind was working at lightning speed. Without hesitation he shoved his gun back into its sheath.

"Hell, no" he agreed. "I'll say I don't. Where you going?"

"To my ranch!" yelled the other as a shotgun boomed through the window opening and buck-

55

shot spattered them with dust. "Come on."

Down the alley they raced with the shotgun booming behind them.

"Got to get my horse!" Hatfield said. "Watson's stable."

"Right around the next corner," panted the dark man. "Hustle, feller, we got to get outa this."

During the run down the alley, Hatfield had made up his mind. These men had no desire to come to grips with the law. Why, he didn't know, but the fact that they didn't want to was important. One of the Lone Wolf's axioms was: "When you're hunting snakes, go where snakes hang out."

Without hesitation he saddled Goldy and led him from the stable. Outside the others were waiting, already mounted, their horses champing impatiently.

"You sure raised Cain, and shoved a chunk under a corner, feller," said the swarthy leader. "Listen to 'em bawl up there!"

"Uh-huh, and you set that hog-waller on fire when you busted those lamps," growled the owner of the deep bass. "Bet you ol' Raines rides out with warrants for all of us tomorrow. Look at 'er blaze!"

"Not a chance," replied the leader. "Casuse, who owns the place, won't make a complaint. He'll just report a fight between jiggers he didn't know. See, they're getting the fire out, too. Well, come on, let's sift sand."

Through a maze of crooked, evil smelling al-

56

leys the swarthy man led the way. Soon the hard, white surface of the trail unrolled before them. Hatfield found himself riding swiftly east. The swarthy man reined back beside him.

"Feller, you're a whizzer with a gun," he admired. "It's none of my business why those hellions wanted to cash you in and I'm not asking the reason. Fact is, I'm asking you just one question — you passing through, or you aiming to hang around these parts for a spell?"

Hatfield tried to read his face, but the moon was now low in the sky and the night too dark.

"All depends," he replied. "I'm sort of trailing my rope at present — out of a job."

"Fine!" exclaimed the other. "I can use a hand like you. Be plumb pleased to sign you up, if you're agreeable."

"All right," Hatfield told him. "I'll give you a whirl. What did you say your outfit is?"

"The Circle P, over to the east," replied the other. "I'm Brant Preston!"

8

Dawn was streaking the sky with rose and gold and flaming scarlet when they reached the white adobe buildings of the Circle P. Thoroughly tired out, the Ranger tumbled into the bunk assigned him in the bunkhouse and went to sleep. The others were not slow in following his example. None of them saw the lithe, furtive man who slipped silently out of the grove back of the ranchehouse, entered the building and soon afterward departed as silently as he had come.

When Jim awoke, Curly Wilkes, the big man with the bass voice, was sitting on the foot of his bunk.

"The Boss wants you to come up to the house," Curly said. "Wants to talk with you. Yeah," in answer to Jim's question, "There's a nice big trough in back you can take a bath in. Go ahead, no women folks around hereabouts. Nice water. I had a bath in there a month come next Saturday; didn't find but three frogs. Nary a snake."

Jim had his bath without disturbing any frogs. Pulling on a swiftly rolled cigarette, he strolled up to the front door of the big white ranch-house.

He found the ranch owner eating breakfast. Preston waved a hospitable hand to a chair on the opposite side of the table.

"Set, and get on the outside of a helping of chuck," he invited. "I just hired a new cook an hour or so ago and he sure knows how to rustle vitals. My last one was a Mex woman with seven kids. She up and marries a widower with nine. Time they get started in business themselves they ought to have a right pert family. Got a good head start, anyhow. The jigger I just took on talks like he's crazy, but scrambles eggs till you think they're just laid this morning, instead of having to be hit with a meat ax to stop them crowin' before you put 'em in the skillet."

The kitchen door opened and a plate of golden eggs and fragrant fried ham came in. With them was a bland Chinaman. Not so bland, however, as when Jim saw him the night before in the Cuevas restaurant. One eye was partially closed and beautifully ringed with blue. His nose was scratched and his lips had a puffy look.

"Howdy," greeted the Ranger mildly. "How come you aren't at the restaurant?"

"Boss clome in without wife," explained the Celestial. "Wife she hit ketchup bottle with me — hit chair with Boss. Me quit before something happen."

"Hell, you look like you didn't quit soon enough. But how come the Boss's wife cut up all this shindig when you just said he came in without her?"

"Boss he clome in front door with red-head dance hall glirl. Boss' wife clome in back door with shotgun. Me say Boss gone before he clome in. She say, 'You liar!' She right!"

"Reckon you did best not to argue with her," agreed Jim. "Say, this ham is sure prime."

"Me cook squeal out pig and make um sweet like music," nodded the Chinaman as he headed for the door.

"I sure believe you could," admitted Preston. "By the way, what's your name, so I can put it on the payroll"

"Me Hang Soon," replied the new cook.

"Wouldn't be a mite surprised," agreed Preston. "Anyhow, you're honest about it. Most folks won't admit it."

He turned to Jim as the Chinaman vanished after more biscuits.

"Got a few things to tell you," he said. "First off, if you sign up with me you're signing up with a somewhat unpopular outfit. Some folks hereabouts ain't got much use for the Circle P. My boys ain't exactly what you'd call daisy pickers. I sort of make it a practice to hire hands that are willing to back the spread up if necessary, but I always tell them what they're up against so they can pull out in time if they've a mind to."

"That's square enough," Jim admitted. "Well, most border outfits are salty; I've worked with one or two myself that didn't go to Sunday school regular. You pay average wages?"

"I pay a little better than most," Preston replied. "There's one other little thing I want to mention," he added, his darkly blue eyes inscrutable, his face wooden in its lack of expression.

"Yeah?"

"Uh-huh — I served a stretch down Mexico way for rustlin'."

"Hell, it's a wonder you come out of it alive; those calabooses aren't health resorts," was Jim's only comment.

For an instant Preston's eyes flickered slightly and a crease appeared between his dark brows. His glance was speculative as it rested on the Lone Wolf's bronzed face. He started to speak, hesitated, and apparently changed his mind. What he did say, Jim felt sure, was not what he had at first intended.

"All right," he said brusquely, "I'll sign you up soon as we finish eating."

Over his cigarette, Jim mentioned that he had encountered Lonnie Garrett and *Don* Fernando Cartina in the course of his ride toward Cuevas, refraining from going into detail as to the meeting.

"That little redhead is sure a pretty girl," he added.

Preston's black brows drew together and there was a smoldering glow in his eyes. He opened his lips and shut them tight again. Once more Jim felt that he did not speak his first thought.

"Yeah, she is," Preston said. "How'd you say you spelled your last name?"

At the door, before going out to the bunkhouse, Hatfield paused.

"Last night when I was amblin' along with *Don*

Fernando's *vaqueros,* I heard them talking about some jigger they called 'The Rider'; seemed all worked up over him. You any notion what they meant?"

For a second time Brant Presto's black lashes flickered. His dark face grew bleak.

"Feller," he said softly, "there's some things in this section that it ain't overly healthy to gab about too much. That there 'Rider' gent is one of 'em."

9

During the next few days Hatfield attended to routine range chores, mostly in the vicinity of the ranchehouse. Somebody always accompanied him and he gained the impression that his fellow workers were covertly studying him the while. They had little to say except as it concerned the work, but were friendly enough. Hatfield gathered that they were summing him up for some definite reason. Curly Wilkes in particular sounded him out in an awkwardly innocent fashion and got exactly nowhere for his pains. All Hatfield did was foster the notion that he was intentionally vague as to his antecedents and noncommittal as to his future.

Hatfield had to admit, in all fairness, that the attitude of the Circle P was not unreasonable. He had been introduced to the spread under rather dubious circumstances. They had undoubtedly approved of his ability to take care of himself in a shindig, but he couldn't blame them for being curious as to just what it was all about. He learned that Preston's need for good hands was desperate. It was a "home guard" section. The spreads were old and established, the riders were not much for changing jobs, and chuck line riding hands were not attracted to the turbulent section. The wandering cowboys tended to keep farther to the north where things were more peaceful and the work less difficult.

He quickly decided that the Circle P was good range despite the proximity of the desert on the east and the hill formations to the north. He learned that Lonnie Garrett's holding was the biggest and best in the section, with that of *Don* Fernando Cartina running second.

"But Cartina is more interested in his mines than in his ranch," Brant Preston told him. "They're his big money makers. He's a first rate cowman, however, and he's got a range boss and general assistant who is tops, even if he is a cross between a sidewinder and a gila monster on the prod.

"Oh, chances are you'll see him the next time you see Cartina," Preston added. "Pierce Kimble is Cartina's shadow. And I'd hate to have a shadow like that following me around."

"You don't seem to think very well of Kimble," Hatfield commented.

"Wait till you see him," Preston replied grimly. He did not elaborate, and Hatfield decided it would be useless to question him further.

Two days later, Hatfield and Wes Crowley rode to town to order supplies for the Circle P's depleted larder.

"We've got a spread of work to do, but just the same I don't favor a man taking that ride alone," Preston explained to Hatfield. "Too many funny things been happening in this section of late and as I told you, there are quite a few folks on the prod against us right now. That Garrett affair

64

didn't do me one bit of good."

Hatfield waited, but still Preston did not see fit to amplify his frequent allusions to what went on in Mexico. Hatfield felt that he would do so in his own good time and no sooner.

They reached town without incident. While Crowley was busy with some personal affairs of his own, Hatfield dropped into a bar for a drink and to do a little thinking. He felt that he had gotten exactly nowhere in the week he had been in the Cuevas country. Everybody seemed willing to talk and say nothing. Hatfield sensed that there was some sort of undercover friction between Brant Preston and the courtly *Don* Fernando Cartina. Perhaps it was due to Preston's pronounced aversion to Pierce Kimble, *Don* Fernando's range boss and chief assistant in running his mines. Preston had said nothing detrimental to Cartina, but Hatfield was sure he had scant use for the ranch and mine owner who appeared to be one of the most influential men in the section.

Sipping his drink, Hatfield gazed into the back bar mirror and saw the very man of whom he had been thinking. But he paid scant heed to *Don* Fernando Cartina, who had just pushed through the swinging doors. His whole attention was centered on the man who glided rather than walked just a little behind the mine owner. Instinctively he knew the man was Pierce Kimble. He turned sideways to get a better look at that unprepossessing individual. As his eyes rested on Hatfield's face, he started visibly and his spear-point hands tensed.

Hatfield's face remained expressionless. He nodded to *Don* Fernando who waved acknowlegement and came forward, a smile of greeting widening his mouth. Pierce Kimble drifted along behind him. Hatfield recalled Brant Preston's "shadow" metaphor.

When he reached the Ranger, Cartina turned to his companion.

"Pierce," he said, "this is Hatfield, the fellow I was telling you about. Understand he signed up with the Circle P since I saw him last."

Pierce Kimble nodded and shook hands. His palm had a clammy feel, but his fingers were like steel wires.

"So you're working for Brant Preston?" he remarked questioningly, his voice a soft burr.

"That's right," Hatfield replied. "He has a nice spread."

"Yes, a nice outfit," said Kimble. Looking the Ranger full in the eyes, he smiled, a slow, creeping smile that twisted his paper-thin lips, lifting them from his sharp, crooked and slightly yellow teeth, wrinkled his dead-colored cheeks, but never reached his jetty eyes. And as that slow smile came and went, Hatfield felt as if a goose were walking over where his grave would be.

"The kind of a grin you get from a rattlesnake when he loops up and looks at you with his tail buzzing," ran through his mind. "Only this reptile wouldn't do any buzzing — not until after he'd struck."

Cartina and Kimble accepted a drink. The former chatted easily with Hatfield, but Kimble was silent until they turned to go. Then —

"Maybe I'll be dropping in to see you and your outfit," he observed with apparent irrelevance. Again he looked Hatfield in the eyes and began his slow smile. Suddenly, however, his lips stiffened and his black gaze faltered. The eyes into which he stared had grown cold as frosted gun muzzles. For a moment he tried to meet the Lone Wolf's icy glance, but something in that glance smashed his lids down as a physical blow. His spear-head hands raised slightly toward the black guns swinging low against his stringy hips, butts to the front, then dropped. Without a word he turned and followed Cartina from the saloon. Hatfield gazed after him, his eyes growing puzzled, retrospective. Hatfield never forgot a face nor any peculiar physical characteristic or action.

"Now where," he murmured, "have I seen that lizard-eyed hellion before. I have, that's sure for certain, and under circumstances that weren't nice, but I'm darned if I know where or when. And I'm willing to bet he's seen me before, too, and recognized me the minute he set eyes on me. That little jerk of his head gave him away. Well, this complicates matters further. Understand he saved Cartina's life once and that Cartina feels mighty grateful to him. Okay, but I'd say having to associate with him is a heavy price to pay for even a life. Maybe it isn't, to Cartina's way of thinking. Where in blazes have I seen him before?"

Humanity is prone to error, and Jim Hatfield, despite his unusual abilities, was no exception to the fixed rule. He instinctively associated the unsavory Kimble with some occurrence in the course of his Ranger activities. Had his mind dropped back some years earlier to college days, when during summer vacations he roamed over Mexico, New Mexico, Arizona, and other places, he might have recalled where he had seen the man who called himself Pierce Kimble, looking younger and considerably different, in action. But he didn't, and because of the oversight his life hung by a frayed thread from that moment on.

And again Hatfield had a vision of a dark, sinister face rushing toward him out of the night.

"Hell!" he muttered disgustedly, "Getting so everybody I see reminds me of that infernal 'Rider'!"

10

Wes Crowley bustled in a little later. With him was a stringy old cowhand with a lined, leathery, but not unpleasant face. He had faded blue eyes that nevertheless had a gleam in their depths. Hatfield noted that he wore a heavy gun slung low against his right thigh. The plain black handle was worn smooth. There were several tiny notches scarring the butt, the significance of which was not lost on the Ranger.

"This is Bob Whetsall," Crowley introduced his companion. "Run into him down at the Ace-Full. He just hit town and is on the lookout for a chore of riding. He's heading back to the spread with us. I got a notion the Boss will be glad to see him. We need men mighty bad."

Hatfield liked the way Whetsall shook hands, and the snag-toothed grin that wrinkled his lips.

"Salty, but real," the Ranger decided.

Whetsall proved to be a cheerful and loquacious soul. As they drank together, Hatfield's liking for the old fellow increased.

"Where'd you spring from, old-timer?" he asked.

"Arizona," Whetsall replied. "Spent most of my life over there around Tombstone and Galeyville. But I got itchy feet and like to roam around. Took a notion to sashay over here. Never been here before. If I'd known it was such a gosh-awful stretched-out section, I wouldn't have come. You don't eat regular, ridin' the chuck line over here. Mighty glad to tie onto a job where there's a table to stick your feet under."

Crowley glanced around quickly. "Rode in Arizona once myself," he announced. "That's where I met Brant Preston. Rode for him before he sold out and moved to Texas. Good range over there, but the droughts are humdingers. A bad one can finish off a spread in a season."

"You're right about that," agreed Whetsall. "Not much water in that section, and if you don't get rain, you're done for."

Crowley wiped his lips with the back of his hand and glanced at the clock.

"Guess we'd better be trailing our twine," he said. "We'll be getting back late as it is, and plenty to do tomorrow. Preston calculates to comb the east brakes tomorrow. And the north pastures have to be gone over, too. Let's go."

Preston was glad to sign Whetsall on. "Once you and Hatfield get the lowdown on the holdings, we'll be in pretty good shape," he announced after the day's work was done and the hands were assembled in the kitchen to do justice to Hang Soon's offerings. "Hatfield, you and Whetsall can hold the fort tonight. I've got a few chores to do in town. I'll take the rest of the boys with me. Getting so a man doesn't dare take a ride without a bodyguard. Damn Pierce Kimble and — and other loco gun slingers.

70

"Kimble hasn't any use for me," he explained apologetically to Hatfield. "And I don't hanker to tangle with him. I'm pretty good, but I know I wouldn't have a chance against that infernal cross-pull of his."

"Cross-pull?" Hatfield repeated. "Don't often see that kind of a draw from a holster."

"That's right," Preston nodded. "But Kimble uses it. Pulls just as if he was dragging across a gun stuck in his belt. You say you saw him the other day? You may have noticed he wears his guns with the butts slung to the front."

Hatfield nodded, and as they left the table, in his eyes was the baffled expression of one who struggles vainly with memory.

While Hatfield and old Bob Whetsall played cards and chatted in the bunkhouse and Hang Soon mended clothes and sang a lugubrious ditty that sounded like a quartette of energetic saw filers at work, there was a meeting in a line cabin to the west. Pierce Kimble, the light from a single smoky bracket lamp flickering across his livid countenance, stood with his back to the wall glaring at four men who sat at a table, their backs to the light, their faces whitish blurs in the shadow of low drawn hatbrims.

"I tell you I'm *not* mistaken," Kimble declared with vicious emphasis. "That big hellion is a Ranger. And now," he added grimly, "I'm telling you something else. He's the Lone Wolf!"

The men at the table jerked in their chairs.

"Good God! Pierce, you *sure* you're right?" exclaimed one, turning slightly so that for an instant a beam of light vaguely outlined his darkly handsome face.

"Yes, I'm sure I'm right!" Kimble spat. "I never forget a face, especially a face like his. I saw him in action once, up around the Guadalupes. He killed three men with three shots, right and left. He's got one of the fastest gunhands in Texas, and he never misses."

"I've a notion you could shade him, Pierce," said the other speaker.

"Yes, I've a notion I could," Kimble agreed. "I don't think the man lives I can't shade on the draw. But he's got something else beside a fast gunhand, something I wouldn't even try to shade. A brain that works like a piece of oiled machinery. I tell you we're on a spot. We've kept nicely covered up so far, but if he's allowed to run around loose, he'll dig us out, sure as hell. He never fails."

"Then," said the other, with grim decision, "he's got to be stopped."

"Right," agreed Kimble, "but it's a chore. It must be done right so that no hint of suspicion is directed toward us. One slip and we're done. You can't expect to get by with some cock-and-bull story as to how it happened. That wouldn't fool Bill McDowell, and if anything happens to his prize lieutenant, McDowell will be looking into the business in person. We're not ready to have a couple of troops of Rangers down here, not yet. Later we won't care. It's got to be done so we won't be called on to explain to Sheriff

Raines or anybody else."

"You don't think he recognized you?"

"No, I don't think so. I don't think he ever saw me before he came here. Remember, I operated before his time — a good ten years back. He didn't see me that day in the Guadalupes. I wasn't mixed up in that shindig, and I took good care to keep in the clear while things were going on. No, I don't think he recognized me the other night. But that isn't overly important, anyhow. He's got to be taken care of, in a way that won't tie things up with us. That's what *is* important."

A tense silence followed. Then the other speaker said —

"I've a notion how it can be done. May cost us something, but will be worth the price."

His glance locked with Kimble's as he spoke, then slid sideways the merest fraction toward the big man seated on his left.

Kimble's slow smile writhed his face. He nodded as if with perfect understanding, evidently pleased.

"Okay," he said, "You're the brains of this outfit, or supposed to be. You take over."

"Curly," Preston told Wilkes the following morning, "check the north pastures today. See if they're worth a combing out for the next shipping herd. Take Hatfield with you and show him the lay of the land up there. The rest of us will work to the east and chances are we'll go to town later. You two can join us there if you get through in time, although that isn't likely."

The north pastures were hard to work and Hatfield and Wilkes made slow progress. Late in the afternoon Wilkes led the way to a clearly defined trail that threaded through gorges and ravine and seemed to always seek the shadow of overhanging cliff or dense thicket. It was a furtive track that shunned the open sunlight and hurried toward the dark shadow of the more northern hills.

"This is the Cingaro Trail," said Wilkes. "There are folks who say the devil swished it out with his tail in the first place. Can't say as to that, but it's sure helped to keep hell working overtime ever since it was first rode. You ever hear tell of it?"

He stared straight at his horse's ears as he spoke, but Hatfield caught the glint of his eyes sliding toward their corners. He replied readily, and with truth.

"Seems that little redhead, Miss Garrett, said something about it when I was riding with her and *Don* Fernando the night I landed in this section," he said. "I never heard of it before. You see, I rode over here from the west. Never before been this far south in this particular section of Texas. Worked last on a spread up in the Silver River country. Used to ride in the Alamita basin and around the Llano River. Was with old man Hogadorn's Hashknife spread in the river country."

Wilkes nodded soberly. "Heard tell of the Hashknife outfit," he admitted. "Salty outfit, I heard. Once knew a feller who worked for Hogadorn."

Hatfield's lips twitched slightly. He knew very well Wilkes was trying to draw him out and had slipped up. Both the Hashknife and Hogadorn were pure figments of the imagination, created on the spur of the moment.

"I rode for a spell in Mexico," he added meaningly. "Rode north mighty fast one day."

Curly Wilkes nodded his understanding and looked pleased. More than one puncher has ridden out of Mexico with a blood feud on his hands. And often as not the feud catches up with him north of the Rio Grande with disastrous results to said puncher.

For some time they rode in silence toward the dark jumble of the hills, Wilkes about twice the length of his horse in the lead. Directly ahead the trail slanted up a long rise to an irregular rim aflare with the saffron flame of the low-lying sun.

From the brush-bristled rim mushroomed a puff of whitish smoke. Hatfield heard the thud of the striking bullet. Even as the spiteful crack of the hidden rifle reached his ears, Wilkes slumped sideways and fell, to lie sprawled and motionless.

For an instant Hatfield sat stunned, automatically jerking his horse to a halt. Then he went out of the saddle like a flash of light, hit the ground and lay prone in the grass. He jerked his rifle from the saddle boot as he fell. With the butt clamped hard against his shoulder, he hammered the glowing rim with bullets where the puff of smoke had rolled upward.

There was no answer to his fire. He emptied

the magazine, stuffed in fresh cartridges and fired three more shots, raking the brush to right and left. The rim remained silent. For minutes he lay tense and ready, then he leaped to his feet, and instantly hurled himself down again. Nothing happened. The rim stretched empty of sound or movement.

Hatfield cast a glance at Curly Wilkes. He lay partly on his side, facing the Ranger. There was a neat blue hole just above his left temple. The whole right side of his head was blown away by the battered emerging slug. Hatfield muttered an oath, stared at the rim a moment longer, and decided to take a chance. He leaped to his feet and ducking and weaving, ran for the shelter of the brush. He reached it without a shot coming from above. Crouching low, taking advantage of every bit of cover, he worked his way swiftly up the long slope. He redoubled his caution as he drew near the rim. Finally he reached the knife-edge summit, straightened up and peered over the lip.

A little distance to the north the trail slithered over the rim, tumbled steeply down the far slope and disappeared into a dark canyon mouth about half a mile distant. Between those gloomy walls the drygulcher had doubtless vanished.

After studying the forbidding terrain for a moment, Hatfield went over the ground. He found where the killer had left his horse. The hoof marks showed worn irons with no peculiarity of marking. Working back to the rim he discovered where the killer had crouched behind a boulder.

On the ground nearby was what he had hoped to find — an exploded cartridge case.

He found more than he had hoped for. Beside the brass shell lay an unfired cartridge. Hatfield examined both with the greatest care. There was a ragged dent in the round percussion cap of the fired cartridge. The cap of the second was unmarked.

Hatfield stared at the two cartridges. "Talk about getting the breaks!" he muttered. "The buzzard's rifle had a defective firing pin. The mark on this exploded shell shows it. He managed to bust the first cartridge and get Wilkes. But the end of the pin broke off and his second try at me was a misfire. He levered the unexploded cartridge out before he realized what had happened. Then he figured he was on a spot and hightailed without even taking time to scoop up these two shells. Now all I've got to do is run down a gent who owns a rifle with a busted firing pin. Considerable of a chore in a section where everybody packs a saddle gun, but it's something, anyhow. Yes, this second slug was intended for me. No doubt about that. Killing Wilkes was no accident. Nobody who knows the first thing about handling a rife could score such a miss at that distance. Wilkes was a dozen feet in front of me. Yes, he picked Wilkes for the first try, me for the second. And if it hadn't been for the busted pin, he'd have gotten me as easily as he did Wilkes. Just a break that's all. Well, it looks like *I'm* on a spot, and I still don't know who in hell to look out for."

He returned to the trail. Wilkes' horse stood patiently beside its master's body. Hatfield picked up the heavy corpse without difficulty and roped it across the saddle. With a last glance around, he mounted and turned back south, leading Wilkes' horse and its grisly burden. The concentration furrow was deep between his bleak brows. He felt he might have to do considerable explaining to the Circle P bunch, and make the explanation stick.

Of necessity, Hatfield rode slowly, accommodating Goldy's gait to that of the awkwardly burdened led horse. There was no such hindrance, however, for another rider who tore along the snaky Cingaro Trail where it turned west through the hills, spuring his racing horse and cursing the rifle in his saddle boot. He also cursed his own neglect.

"I knew that pin was loose," he told himself with vicious emphasis. "This is what I get for putting off having it fixed. A prime chance gone haywire. Now I'll have to put Pedro and Miguel on the job. Think I've got time." He glanced at the sun, the lower edge of which was just touching the crests of the more distant hills, made a quick mental calculation. "Yes, I got time, if I hustle," he muttered. "*They* won't slip. Blast them, they'd better not!"

A few minutes later he turned off the main trail and rode south by a little west.

11

Old John Doan, driver of the Crater-Cuevas stage, heaved a sigh of relief as the clumsy coach rolled out of shadowy Lobo Canyon and onto the fairly open stretch of desert that lay between the Zarzal Hills and the Cuevas rangeland. Bert Livesay, the shotgun guard, also felt better. In the stage strongbox was the payroll for the Cuevas mines and other specie totalling more than thirty thousand dollars. Of course, the shipment from Crater to the Cuevas bank was made in the strictest secrecy, but you never could tell. Lobo Canyon was an ideal spot for a holdup. Out in the open, with the trail winding clear ahead and only an occasional grove or clump of mesquite to break the monotony, was much better.

"Figure I can take time out for a smoke," remarked Livesay, reaching for "the makin's." Old John rumbled something unintelligible, his deepset gray eyes on the trail ahead. Livesay had half finished his cigarette when the driver grunted sharply.

"Somethin' alongside the road this side that clump of mesquite," he said.

Livesay saw it too, a crouching something that at first puzzled him.

"Hell," he exclaimed suddenly, "It's a dead horse and a couple of fellers. See, one of 'em's layin' on the ground and the other's bendin' over him. Looks like somebody's been hurt."

"Looks that way," agreed the driver, "but we ain't takin' no chances. Get that scattergun of yours handy."

Livesay cocked his shotgun and laid it across his knees. He peered sharply at the queer group as the stage sped down the low rise. It was but a hundred yards distant when the crouching figure turned.

"Look!" exclaimed Livesay, "He *is* hurt — all covered with blood."

The man's face was a bloody smear. The features were indistinguishable as such. He swayed on his knees and tried to stagger erect. They could now see that the man who lay prone on his back was also covered with blood. The horse that lay by the side of the road had a broken leg, the white splintered bone protruding through the skin. A little distance away another horse stood with hanging head and widespread feet, apparently in the last stages of exhaustion.

Old John's hand tightened on the reins. The kneeling man opened his bloody mouth.

"Help!" he croaked. "Help!" and collapsed across the motionless body of his companion.

Throwing his weight against the reins, old John pulled the stage to a jingling halt. His passengers, two elderly drummers, peered through the window with anxious faces.

"You keep an eye on things," John told the guard. "I'll see what I can do for those fellers."

He got down stiffly and stumped forward. Stooping over the injured man he tried to lift him from the flaccid body of his companion, but the weight was too great for his strength.

"Give me a hand, Bert," he called. "This one 'pears to be still alive — the other one's just *soaked* with blood."

Livesay laid his shotgun on the seat and swung down. The unconscious man was groaning pitifully. His companion lay without sound or movement. Livesay bent down to assist Doan.

Like a released spring, the "injured" man came to his feet. His fist crashed against the old driver's jaw and knocked him down. Livesay, astounded recognition popping his eyes and sagging his jaw, went for his gun. The "dead" man on the ground was galvanized into instant action. His hand flickered like a striking snake and he shot from the hip, smashing the guard in the stomach and breast with heavy slugs. Livesay went down, gasping and retching. Old John Doan was struggling to his feet. A bullet took him squarely between the eyes and he crumpled up beside the dying guard.

The terror-stricken passengers heard the drum of swift hoofs. From the mesquite thicket down the trail burst two riders, one leading a spare horse. They swept up to the stage, their eyes glinting through the holes in the black masks they wore.

"Haul that box out," one curtly ordered the two passengers. He swung to the ground as the trembling men hastened to obey. From his saddlebags he took a hammer and a cold chisel. A few blows knocked the lid off the box. Working with swift efficiency, the four robbers transferred the gold and bills from the box to their saddlebags.

"All right," the leader told the passengers, "if either of you can drive, you can take this contraption to town. If you can't, you'll have to wait till somebody comes along and picks you up. *Adios!*"

Securing the shotgun, rifle and sixes of the slain guard and driver, the grim quartette mounted, the "injured" man forking the exhausted horse which was not nearly so exhausted as it appeared. Without a glance at their murdered victims they rode into the dark mouth of Lobo Canyon.

The taller of the two passengers spoke in a quavering voice —

"S-see that dead horse! Its throat has been cut. That's where they got the blood to smear on their faces. God, I'm sick!"

His companion, of a sterner mold, walked over to the silent bodies.

"Come on and help me put them in the coach," he said. "I can drive a little, enough to keep this damn hearse on the road. Hurry, it's nearly dark."

12

Night had long fallen when Hatfield reached the Circle P. The bunkhouse was dark and a single light showed where Hang Soon pottered about the ranchhouse kitchen. It was very shadowy under the trees that shaded the bunkhouse.

Hatfield dismounted, and taking Curly Wilkes' stiffening body in his arms, headed for the bunkhouse. The door was ajar; he kicked it open and entered. He tensed as he thought he glimpsed a stealthy movement.

Out of the dark interior gushed a lance of flame; the walls rocked to the roar of a gun. Hatfield reeled back under the terrific impact of the heavy slug; his heel caught on the door sill and he sprawled on the ground. Through the doorway leaped two shadowy figures hissing exultant curses.

Prone on the ground, the Lone Wolf drew and fired from the hip, the explosions of his gun blending in a single deafening roar of sound.

The foremost figure crumpled up like a sack of old clothes. The second man yelled in shrill agony as he went down. Whirling over sideways, Hatfield drew his other gun and grimly hammered the prostrate forms with bullets. Then he got stiffly to his feet, lean face set, eyes bleakly cold.

Inside the ranchhouse he could hear Hang Soon's squalling screeches and the scampering of his slippered feet.

"Bring a light, Hang," he shouted. "It's me, Hatfield. Rustle a hoof!"

"Me bling shotgun!" howled Hang. "Me blow loose' flom under hat!"

"You leave that scattergun be!" roared Hatfield. "If you start pulling trigger the only safe place'll be behind you!"

"Me turn 'lound quick!" squealed Hang. "Me glet um behind in flont!"

A moment later he came pattering through the door with a lantern, muttering something that sounded like firecrackers going off in a rain barrel.

The Ranger took the lantern, but he did not first turn to the two men he had shot; he felt reasonably sure they would stay where they were. Instead he bent over the grotesquely sprawled form of Curly Wilkes.

There was a hole in Curly's chest now in addition to the one between his glazed eyes, a futile looking hole from which no blood oozed. A whitish glimpse of shattered breastbone showed.

"Lucky for me the slug hit him in the thickest part," Hatfield told himself grimly. "If I hadn't had him up in my arms in front of me, both he and I would be lying down saying nothing. Reckon it was so dark under the trees the hellions didn't notice two horses. Grass is mighty thick and they couldn't tell from hearing that two sets of hoofs were working. Guess when they saw me tumble backward they thought they'd done for me. Wonder if they were waiting for me or somebody else?

"Let's see if we can find where they left their horses," he remarked to the chattering Chinaman. "Where is everybody?"

"Whetsall he ride night guard on herd combed out over east," said Hang. "Boss-man Preston, Hilton, Kearns, and Crowley ride town."

Hatfield nodded. "Let's see —" he began, and suddenly tensed.

"Horse what ain't here come," gurgled Hang Soon apprehensively.

"Uh-huh, coming fast, too. Douse that lantern and get back out of sight under the trees."

Hang Soon hastened to obey. Hatfield glided to his horse and pulled his heavy rifle from the boot. Hidden in the shadows he waited, his eyes on the trail that leaped from the blackness of a grove a few hundred yards distant. Moonlight was flooding it now and it glowed like cooling liquid silver.

Four horsemen burst from the grove and rode swiftly toward the ranchhouse. Hatfield peered with narrowed eyes, noting that the coats of the animals were dark with sweat and flecked with patches of foam. He stepped from the shadows and called a greeting. A moment later Brant Preston and his three cowboys, Crowley, Kearns and Hilton, were dismounting in front of the bunkhouse.

"What the blazes is going on?" demanded the Circle P owner. "We heard shootin' and hustled to get here."

Hatfield told them, briefly, with no waste of words. As he related the circumstances of Curly Wilkes' death, he read suspicion and distrust in the hard eyes of the three punchers. Preston's dark face was inscrutable. When Hatfield had finished, Preston knelt down and examined the body of Wilkes by the lantern which Hang Soon had relighted. He gave particular attention to the head wound. Finally he nodded and got to his feet.

"Judging from what I've seen of folks that's been shot, and I've seen quite a few, poor old Curly got his brains blown loose in just about the way you mentioned," he said. "He was shot by somebody from quite a ways off and up above him using a big calibre rifle, I'd say. No doubt about that other wound being gotten after he was dead. Now does anybody know these devils Hatfield perforated?"

"They're breeds," said Crowley, a grim, taciturn little man with a drooping moustache.

"Mostly Indian blood," amended gangling, lantern-jawed Hank Hilton. "Nope, I ain't seen neither of 'em before. Have you, Tart?"

Tart Kearns, whose mild blue eyes were as deceptive as was his slight frame, shook his head wordlessly. Tart seldom said anything, but when he did it was listened to.

"You can see what you've let yourself in for,

Hatfield," remarked Brant Preston a trifle wearily. "Wilkes makes the third man I've had killed in the past two months — and never knew who did the killing. This is the first time we've ever even seen hide or hair of any of the hellions."

"Maybe this'll end it — maybe these are the jiggers that have been kicking up all the hell," Hatfield offered tentatively.

Preston swore a deep-cheated oath. "No chance," he growled. "These skulking skunks are just a couple of hired hands. There's somebody else back of this — somebody with brains."

Wes Crowley drawled what seemed an utterly irrelevant remark —

"I saw Pierce Kimble and Fernando Cartina in town last night. They grinned at me."

Again Hatfield sensed a sudden stiffening of the group. Preston's voice broke harshly on the silence —

"Wes, you know nobody's got anything against Kimble that would connect him with such doings as this. He's a killer, and the fastest gun slinger in these parts, but that don't mean the feller's a thief and a murderer."

"I got no use for that dead-faced tarantula and I never will have," Crowley declared, "and when he grins at me, that slow, creepin' grin of his, I get the shivers."

Hatfield glanced swiftly at the hardbitten little man. He had a feeling that all Wes Crowley knew about fear was the murky idea conveyed to him by the dictionary definition, that is, if Wes had ever seen the inside of a dictionary, which he doubted.

The group shifted uncomfortably at Crowley's words. Even the more intelligent Preston seemed ill at ease. He spoke hurriedly, with an evident desire to change the subject.

"The sheriff'll have to know about these killings," he said. "If we don't say anything about 'em it'll look suspicious. We could pitch the breeds in a hole and it would be all right, but folks are going to ask questions about Curly not showing up no more. We can't afford to have folks talk. Somebody'll have to ride to town tonight and tell Jed Raines what happened."

There was a swift interchange of glances, but nobody volunteered for the mission. Preston, hesitantly, turned to Hatfield.

"Hatfield," he said, "your horse looks pretty fresh and ours have had a hard day. The boys are all about tuckered out, too. You mind riding to town and telling the sheriff what happened?"

"Not at all," Hatfield replied instantly. He noted relief on the part of the others.

"Grab yourself a bite to eat while we put our cayuses up," Preston said. "Come on, boys, these bronks need some looking after before they're bedded down. Hank, take Curly's feet first and we'll lay him in his bunk till the sheriff gets here. Leave them two hydrophobia skunks where they are."

Hatfield slipped the rig off Goldy and let him roll. "I'll give him a helpin' of oats while you eat," Hilton offered.

Half an hour later, Hatfield was riding swiftly toward Cuevas. The others were still busy in the barn with their horses.

The concentration furrow was deep between the Ranger's black brows as the big sorrel's hoofs clicked on the trail. He had plenty to think about, for he had an uneasy suspicion that his story had not been wholly believed by the Circle P bunch. They were taking an undue amount of time to attend to the simple wants of the sturdy horses. The cayuses had been ridden hard but were certainly in no distress. A quick rubdown was all any of them needed. It was plain to Hatfield that they wanted him out of the way while they discussed the recent happenings. At the moment he was sure a hot argument was raging. As would be expected from a man familiar with gunshot wounds, Preston's diagnosis of the fashion in which Curly Wilkes met his death was accurate. But Hatfield felt he had deliberately evaded the indubitable fact that Wilkes could have very easily met death at the hands of the man who companioned him on the checking chore in the hills. Two hands checking cattle do not stick together all the time. And he, Hatfield, would have had ample opportunity to kill Wilkes in just the fashion he had been killed. Perhaps they had not believed a word he said and were even now discussing what action to take.

But what about the two breeds who had attempted to drygulch him in the bunkhouse? The incident should puzzle Preston and his men. And it lent credence to his explanation of the death of Wilkes. Hatfield figured that the murder attempt by the breeds was the only thing that had saved him immediate and serious trouble with Preston and his hands, trouble that would have forced him to reveal his Ranger connections.

Not for an instant did he doubt that the two attempts on his life were inspired by the same source. Some clear, cold brain, knowing the first attempt had failed, had instantly and shrewdly arranged a second. And again he had gotten the breaks. Had he not been packing Wilkes' body against his breast, *he* would have received the slug.

Hatfield's keen eyes missed little and he never underestimated the value of small and seemingly inconsequential details, especially if they were out of the orderly routine. At the moment he was wondering why saddle pouches had been added to the Circle P's rigs. The flapping things are a nuisance to a rider and are never worn during ordinary range work. Of course, he understood, Preston and his bunch had been to town. They might have added the leather bags to their riding equipment in anticipation of packing articles back to the ranch. The bags had been filled, all right, well plumped out. Otherwise he might not have noticed them in the uncertain light. The incident was doubtless of no significance, but Hatfield noted it.

It was long after midnight when he reached Cuevas and the town was still going full blast. He shouldered his way to a bar and asked where he could locate the sheriff.

"His office is just around the corner, two streets up," said the barkeep. "You won't find him there, though," he added as he poured Hatfield a drink. "He's out chasin' the jiggers that held up the stage and shot the driver and the guard. Yeah, they made a good haul — the payroll for the mines. It was bein' brought to the Cuevas bank from Crater — all in gold. The stage was held up over to the northeast of here, other side of that strip of desert, just before dark, by four mighty salty *hombres!*"

13

Hatfield stood quietly sipping his drink as the bartender attended to the wants of another customer. He was waiting for further details. The barkeep came back in a few minutes, and took up where he had left off.

"None of the passengers could tell what they looked like?" Hatfield asked, after the drink juggler had finished his story.

"Nope. Two of the hellions were masked and the other two had blood or red paint smeared all over their faces till they looked like Indians. Guess the passengers were too scared to see anything straight, anyhow. Bert or John might have seen something, but they were both dead. Maybe the sheriff'll get them. Stick around here if you want to see him, he'll be sure to come here for a drink soon as he gets in — always does. Here, have one on the house while you're waiting."

Jim took his drink to a nearby table and sat down to wait for the sheriff. The room was not so crowded now for it was getting along toward morning. He ran his eyes over the scattering of men drinking at the bar or gambling and saw no one he knew. Suddenly his glance centered on the swinging doors, a man was just coming through them whose face *was* familiar. A moment later he recognized *Don* Fernando Cartina.

The ranch owner saw him at the same instant and came over to the table. He nodded a greeting and sat down wearily.

"*Tequilla,*" he told the waiter who hurried up for his order.

Hatfield returned the nod and his gaze ran over Cartina. The latter's hat and clothes were powdered with reddish dust. His face had a tired look and there were dark circles under his eyes.

"Has the sheriff got back yet?" he asked. "Reckon you've heard about the robbery?

"The payroll for my mine was in that strongbox," he went on as Hatfield nodded. "I don't stand to lose anything, of course. The money was still in charge of the bank, but it confuses things and I had to come in to make arrangements. One of my men was in town and heard about what had happened. He hustled right out to the ranch with the news and my range boss, Pierce Kimble, and I rode straight into town. Just got here."

"Barkeep said the sheriff would be sure to stop here when he got in," Hatfield offered.

"I'll wait a bit," replied Cartina. "I've got to look up Darnel, the bank cashier, and see what he can do about the payroll." His eyes grew thoughtful. "I can't help but feel that it would have been better if you had signed up with some other spread, Hatfield," he remarked. "The Circle P is a turbulent outfit and lots of people around here don't think any too well of them.

Not that they have ever been suspected of any specific wrongdoing," he hastened to add.

"You can't be too choosy when you need a job," Hatfield replied.

"That's so," admitted *Don* Fernando. "Well, ride out to my place whenever you get time. You take the first trail to the north after you pass out of town heading west. Can't lose your way. It's a plain trail across the grassland all the way."

Hatfield's face did not change, but there was a slight glow in the depths of his level eyes.

"Grassland all the way? Plain trail across it?"

"Yes," replied Cartina. "Easy to follow — ten mile ride."

For some time after they sat sipping their drinks and saying little.

"I'm waiting for Pierce," *Don* Fernando observed at length. "He went to put the horses away and see if the sheriff was in his office. I think a lot of Pierce Kimble," he added. "He saved my life once."

"That's apt to make you think sort of well of a feller," Hatfield admitted.

Hatfield rolled and lighted a cigarette. Cartina sipped his drink and continually glanced at the door. He seemed nervous and ill at ease about something.

"Here he comes now," he exclaimed a few minutes later, relief in his voice. Hatfield wondered why he should worry about the self-sufficient Kimble.

As he drew near, Kimble shot a questioning

glance at *Don* Fernando who nodded slightly. Kimble seemed to settle into himself as if *he* were relieved about something. His murky eyes swept across Hatfield's face and surveyed all corners of the room. Kimble evidently liked to know who was around before he turned his back. Hatfield was not surprised. He noted that Kimble's head was always slanted a little.

"A 'listening man'," the Ranger mused. "Always 'listening' for a dead man to whisper over his shoulder." He decided to try a little experiment. He casually shifted his position until he was a little behind Kimble. Instantly the other shifted also so that the Ranger was within the scope of his vision. The move was automatic, for he was talking to *Don* Fernando at the time.

Hatfield shifted a little more, then again and still again. Finally he was facing in the opposite direction from when he started moving. *But* — he was still looking into Pierce Kimble's death-mask face. Kimble would *not* allow a companion to get behind him. Hatfield was interested. He had seen *that* before, too, a gesture habitual to men always alert and watchful against the vengeance that ever dogged their heels.

Cartina glanced at the clock. "Well, we'll be leaving you," he said. "I want to rouse up Darnel and then head back for the spread. Ride over and see me some time."

"Okay, I will," Hatfield promised. "Trail right across the rangeland all the way, I believe you said."

"That's right. Grassland trail, easy to ride. Well, so long."

The strangely assorted pair left the saloon. Hatfield gazed after them. In his eyes was again the perplexed look of one who struggles with memory, but his jaw was grimly set, his lips tight. For Fernando Cartina had lied when he said he had ridden straight from his ranchhouse to town. By his own admission, the trail to his spread was a grassland trail. But his clothes and those of Kimble had been thickly powdered with reddish dust, dust that could have only come from the surface of the wide strip of desert between Cuevas and Crater.

"And the stage was held up east of the desert," Hatfield mused. "Now I wonder?"

14

The dawn sky was blushing as pink as the cheek of a girl before Sheriff Jed Raines showed up. He was weary, sweat stained, and reddish dust lay thick in the folds of his rusty coat, but his big shoulders were square and he held himself stiffly erect. Jim liked the grim old face with its frosty gray eyes and its bristling moustache. Behind him shambled his stoop-shouldered, gawky deputy whose soft brown eyes and mild voice had been the undoing of more than one badman not blessed with keenness of perception.

Hatfield walked over to meet the sheriff. Raines looked at him questioningly.

"I'd like to have a word with you, Sheriff, if you aren't too tired," Hatfield requested deferentially. Old Jeb bristled.

"Who said I was tired!" he growled. His chill glance ran over the Ranger's tall form.

"Appears to me you mightily resemble the feller that kicked up the ruckus in Casuse's *cantina* the other night," he remarked.

Hatfield noticed the deputy walk casually past him and bit back a grin with difficulty.

"Uh-huh," he admitted, "wouldn't be surprised if I do look sort of like that feller."

The sheriff's jaw dropped slightly. Hatfield went on before he had time to speak; "You see,

Sheriff, I'm working for Brant Preston of the Circle P."

Jed Raines' jaw snapped back tight, his eyes glowed angrily.

"There was a little trouble out there yesterday," Hatfield continued quickly. "It was like this —"

Tersely he outlined the happenings at the Circle P. "Preston figured you ought to know about it — thought maybe you might want to investigate," he finished.

"Yeah, I reckon I will," grunted the sheriff. "And I reckon I'll want to investigate you a bit, too, young feller."

His glance was over the Ranger's shoulder as he spoke and Hatfield was not in the least surprised to feel a cold circle jammed against the small of his back. Still struggling with the grin, he raised his hands to the level of his shoulder before the deputy could even drawl his mild, "Elevate!"

"You're showin' some sense, anyhow," Raines grunted, relieving Hatfield of his hardware. "All right, out the front door and don't try nothin' funny. You're pretty husky, but this old shootin' iron of mine is a spread sight huskier. Just take it easy and stay healthy."

The big room was in an uproar, but a glance from the sheriff's cold eyes quelled the tumult to a hum. Nobody followed them through the swinging doors.

In front of the sheriff's office, which was the

front room of the little jail, the deputy held the prisoner until Jed Raines got a light going. Then he marched Jim into the office. Here Raines searched him thoroughly, the deputy lounging easily by the door. He felt under Jim's arms for shoulder holsters and at the back of his neck for a possible knife. Finally he stepped back.

"All right, guess you're clean," he grunted. "You can put your hands down."

Hatfield complied. "But you did overlook something important, Sheriff," he remarked mildly.

"Huh!" barked the sheriff, his hand jerking to his holster.

"If you promise not to plug me while I'm doing it, I'll get it for you," Hatfield said.

"I won't promise," growled the sheriff, "but go ahead."

Hatfield loosened his broad leather belt and fumbled with a cunningly concealed secret pocket. He held out his hand. Behind him he heard Hipless Harley, the deputy, chuckle.

Sheriff Raines stared at what Hatfield held in his sinewy palm. His jaw dropped, his eyes bulged. It was a *gleaming silver star set on a silver circle,* the feared and honored badge of the Texas Rangers.

"What the devil!" exploded the sheriff, adding incredulously, "you trying to tell me you're a Ranger?"

"Figure to be," Hatfield replied soberly. "Captain McDowell told me I might have trouble making you see it. He said your eyesight is pretty bad and that you were behind the door when they handed out brains."

"What!" roared the sheriff, his moustache bristling in his scarlet face. "Why, that stove-up, spavined old coot! When I see *him*, I'll work him over till folks won't be able to tell him from a green hide!"

"Uh-huh," agreed Hatfield, plainly not impressed. "Captain Bill recalled the time he dropped you in a trough of sheep dip for arguing with him."

"He didn't!" bawled the sheriff. "My foot slipped."

"Uh-huh, both feet, or so I understand," Hatfield replied dryly. "But he did say you were mighty heavy handling."

A grin creased the old sheriff's leathery countenance. His eyes twinkled.

"Guess in those days Bill McDowell was about the strongest cowhand in south Texas," he remarked reminiscently, "but I gave him a tussle, son, I gave him a tussle! So he did get my letter. Where's the rest of your troop — keepin' under cover?"

"Guess I'm all there is," Hatfield replied. "Captain Bill didn't have a troop to spare."

The sheriff got mad again. "That old fuzzy-brain," he yelped. "He sends me one Ranger! Why, he —"

"Jed," interrupted Hipless Harley, "I guess you got all the troop you need. Don't you know who you're talkin' to? *That's the Lone Wolf!*"

Again the sheriff's jaw dropped. He stared, almost in awe, at the man who was already a legend throughout the Southwest.

"Is — is that right?" he managed at length.

"Of course it's right," said Hipless. "I recognized him the minute I set eyes on him. I'd seen him before."

"Why the blazes didn't you say so, 'stead of lettin' me make a fool of myself?" the sheriff demanded indignantly.

"Figured *he'd* do the sayin' when he was ready," Hipless returned composedly.

"Guess you're right," admitted the sheriff, somewhat mollified. "Sit down, Hatfield. Here's your guns. Hipless, draw them shades and lock the door. What have you learned, Hatfield?"

"Exactly nothing," Hatfield admitted. "And I've been shot at so many times I feel lonesome if I don't hear lead whistling past. A jigger called *The Rider* opened the ball the night I landed in this section."

The sheriff swore luridly. Hipless wagged his head and clucked.

"I'll start at the beginning," Hatfield said. He tersely related, in detail, his experiences since his arrival in the Cuevas Valley country.

Raines swore some more. "It's gettin' worse all the time," he declared. "Take that payroll robbery today, for instance. Two cold-blooded killin's. They could just as easily have thrown down on the driver and the guard, disarmed them, and let them go about their business after they cleaned out the stage. But no, they drilled 'em dead center without givin' them a chance. And that's the way things have been going in recent months. It's a snake-blooded outfit for fair. Why, Curly Bill Graham and his bunch of hellions over in Arizona were no worse than the gang operatin' here. Graham and his bunch were cold killers, but men like John Ringo and the Clanceys and Jim Hill would sometimes give a feller a break. Of course, Graham himself was plumb pizen and deadly as a rattler, but the rest sort of held him down. But there doesn't seem to be anybody in the bunch over here that has a streak of decency in him. The things they've been doing to the poor devils who live in the River villages would set your hair on end just to hear about 'em. I ain't got much use for oilers, no matter which side of the River they live on, but they've got their rights and should be treated as human beings. And you say you haven't learned a thing?"

"Nothing that definitely ties anybody up," Hatfield replied. "But I have decided it is a well disciplined, compact outfit, and a big one. And I'd say all the faces I've managed to get a glimpse of have belonged to breeds, with Yaqui Indian blood predominating. Yaquis as Yaquis are all right. Dangerous to fool with, but pretty decent folks. But for some reason or other, when you mix their blood with white, all too often all the vices of both races are retained with the virtues absent."

Raines nodded gloomy agreement.

"And now," said Hatfield, "I want to ask a few questions about the folks I've met here. I'll begin with Brant Preston and his bunch. What do you know about them?"

Raines tugged his mustache. "Well," he said, "it's a swallerforkin', trouble-makin' outfit. They're always on the prod about something. There were a few more of 'em, but several have gotten knocked off, one way or another. I've never been able to drop a loop on anybody responsible for the killings. Preston swears they were killed from ambush, which could be. An outfit like that makes enemies."

"Plenty of outfits like that in Texas," Hatfield interpolated.

"Uh-huh," the sheriff agreed. "Too darn many, and they don't make it easy for peace officers. I wish this particular one had stayed in Arizona. Not that there's ever been anything off-color tied up with the Circle P," he hastened to add. "Folks have looked sideways at Preston, however, ever since the trouble down in Mexico when Preston was the only one to get back to Texas. Tom Garrett was mighty popular in this section and plenty of folks say Preston should have brought him back or stayed down there with him. It was a fool's business, goin' down there in the first place into Cheno's hole-in-the-wall country. Maybe Preston couldn't bring Garrett back. He swears he did the best he could, even to takin' Garrett along when he busted out of Cheno's jail. But

Garrett was caught again and locked up, while Preston got away. Lonnie Garrett is bitter against Preston, although she used to be sort of friendly with him. But maybe Preston isn't gettin' a fair break. I just don't know."

Hatfield nodded and was silent for a moment.

"And what about Fernando Cartina?" he asked.

The sheriff hesitated. "Cartina seems to be a nice feller," he replied slowly, "even if he does hire only *vaqueros* to do his ridin' for him. But he 'pears to like the notion of keepin' a snake for a pet."

"You mean Pierce Kimble?"

"Yes. He's a reptile if I ever saw one."

"Ever been outside the law?"

"Not that I ever heard of," the sheriff admitted. "But I'd be willin' to bet he has been in his time."

"Suspicion is one thing, proof is another," Hatfield remarked.

"That's right," agreed the sheriff. "No, Kimble has never done anything since he showed up here that would put him on the wrong side of the fence — legally. But he has killed four men in the past two years in self defense."

Something in the way the sheriff said it caused Hatfield to repeat, interrogatively —

"In self defense?"

"Yes. Kimble always let the other fellow clear leather before he even reached. A dozen witnesses could swear, each time, that he shot to

104

save his own life. But they were cold-blooded killings, just the same. There ain't no *defense* against Pierce Kimble when he reaches for a gun. He's got far and away the fastest gunhand I ever saw, and I've seen quite a few in my time. And he's got a way of talkin' that makes folks bust a cinch and go loco as a 'Patchy buck full of red-eye. You can count on it, he taunted those fellers into goin' for their guns."

Hatfield nodded thoughtfully. "I've seen that sort," he replied. "They're plumb bad. Got the killer instinct — always itching to pull trigger. By the way, Cartina and Kimble were in town tonight. Cartina said they rode straight to town from his ranchhouse after one of his men came in and told him about the robbery. He lied."

"Lied? How do you know that?" asked the sheriff.

"They had dust on their clothes." Hatfield replied. "And Cartina told me twice the trail to his *casa* runs over grassland all the way."

"But a man can get dust on his clothes riding a trail over grassland," protested the sheriff.

"Not red dust," Hatfield differed. "Where in this section could a man get red dust on his clothes?"

"Only on the desert over to the east," replied the sheriff. "Red soil over there."

"So I judged from what I saw of the edge of it, riding the Circle P east pasture," Hatfield said. "And the desert lies between here and Crater, doesn't it?"

The sheriff stared. "You mean to say you're accusin' Cartina and Kimble of pullin' that holdup?" he asked.

"I'm accusing nobody," Hatfield replied. "But for some reason known best to himself, Cartina saw fit to lie about where he'd been riding tonight. I believe those drummers said four men took part in the holdup. Wasn't that right?"

"That's right," muttered the sheriff. "But Cartina has a lot of oilers ridin' for him. Now I wonder? It don't make sense, but I wonder?"

"Don't wonder too much," Hatfield cautioned. "It's easy to fix suspicion on anybody if something seems to tie up with the known facts. For that matter, Brant Preston and three of his men were out riding tonight, too. Yet it doesn't mean that they pulled the holdup. By the way, was it generally known that the payroll money would be on the stage?"

"No, it was not," the sheriff declared emphatically. "It was supposed to be a dead secret. The money was supposed to come in by buckboard yesterday. The buckboard, with three guards, did pack a strongbox filled with rocks. The box was delivered to the bank. Plenty of folks saw it carried in. That was supposed to be a trick to fool anybody with designs on the dinero. Then the real box was carried into the stage after dark."

"Would Cartina have known the box was really on the stage?" Hatfield asked.

"Of course," replied the sheriff. "It was the

payroll money for his mines. But just for the sake of the argument, why would Cartina steal his own money?"

"It wasn't his money," Hatfield pointed out. "Not until it was delivered to him. The Crater and Cuevas banks were responsible. It was their money till Cartina received it and signed his receipt."

The sheriff swore again. "I don't know what to think," he said.

"Don't think anything, yet," Hatfield advised. "I'm just showing you how things stand. We don't really know a thing."

"And it looks like we've got a lizard's chance of learnin' anything," the sheriff growled pessimistically.

"Don't be too sure," Hatfield said. "The owl-hoot brand tip their hands, as a rule, by some little slip." He fingered the empty shell and the unfired cartridge in his pocket as he spoke. He hadn't seen fit to tell the sheriff about them yet.

"What about the River villages?" he asked suddenly.

"Scared stiff, and with reason," the sheriff replied. "Of late they've gone sullen and won't talk. Used to be, I could ride along there anytime and it was '*Buenas dias, Señor* Sheriff!' Now they just glower and say nothing."

Hatfield's face was grave. "That's serious," he said. "It looks like somebody is deliberately stirring up the villages."

Raines nodded. "Looks that way," he admitted.

"And suppose the villagers really go on the prod?"

"They could make plenty of trouble," the sheriff said. "There's seven thousand of 'em on this side of the River and another thirty-five thousand or so on the Mexican side. They're all tied up by intermarriage and such. But who in blazes would want to stir 'em up, and why?"

"I don't think the problem is a very obscure one," Hatfield replied. "Porfirio Diaz is none too secure in his Presidency in Mexico. A well planned revolution might easily unseat him."

"It would take an army to do it," scoffed Raines. "And the villagers wouldn't be an army. They'd just be a mob."

"A mob can become an army with training and arms," Hatfield pointed out.

"Uh-huh," agreed the sheriff, "but arms cost money."

"Well," Hatfield countered dryly "from what Captain Bill told me, somebody has been latching onto quite a few thousands hereabouts during the past six months."

"You're right," said Raines. "Why the Cuevas bank robbery and that holdup yesterday counted for better than eighty thousand, and there have been others. The cows they've rustled run into big money. But suppose you're right, who's back of it — Cheno?"

Hatfield shook his head. "I don't think so," he answered. "I'd say somebody with a lot more brains and imagination than Cheno. Perhaps

108

somebody using Cheno for a front. By the way, who's *El Hombre?*"

The sheriff threw out his hands in disgust. "Might as well ask me who are the *Riders*," he growled. "Some folks think Cheno and *El Hombre* are the same. Me, I think there isn't any *El Hombre*. He's just a name to scare the village *peons* with."

"Don't be too sure," Hatfield counselled. "The whole business doesn't seem to make sense and when something doesn't seem to make sense, it'll stand investigating. That sounds paradoxical, I know, but it's true."

"You talk like a dictionary," grumbled the sheriff, "but I reckon I get what you mean. Who do you think *El Hombre* is?"

"I don't," Hatfield smiled, "but I hope to find out. I've a notion if we can learn who *The Man* is, we'll be in shape to drop our loop and clean up this whole business."

"Maybe," said the sheriff, "but gettin' back to the revolution business. I don't see as it makes much difference to us up here who runs the government down there. If they want to revolt, let 'em revolt."

"No, perhaps it doesn't make much difference in theory who runs Mexico," Hatfield countered. "But if such an uprising should occur, inspired and directed by such men as Cheno and *El Hombre,* the Border would be blood and flame from the Gulf to the Pacific. And that makes considerable difference to us up here. Some day," he added prophetically, "a man will arise down there, a man of the people who will purge Mexico of her wrongs, and after him will come a free, prosperous and powerful Mexico that will be a staunch friend and ally of America in her hour of need. Perhaps we won't live to see it, but it will come. But the man will not be of the Cheno and *El Hombre* brand. They aren't concerned with the welfare of Mexico. They just aim to feather their own nests and they won't be particular as to whom they pluck the feathers from."

"Feller, the way you talk, you give me the creeps," growled Raines.

"You'll have more than creeps if we don't get to the bottom of this business in a hurry," Hatfield grimly predicted. "Incidentally, where was Cartina from originally?"

"Right here," said the sheriff. "Grandfather was born the other side of the River, but his father was born in Texas. Sebastian Cartina married an Arizona girl whose folks came from Scotland, I believe. She was a widow, I heard. Fernando Cartina was the result. After his dad died, he and his mother spent a lot of time in Arizona with her folks. When she died, Fernando came back to the old Cartina home place here in Texas. He'd been away several years."

Hatfield nodded thoughtfully. "And Brant Preston came from Arizona, didn't he?"

"That's right, a couple of years back. Owned a spread over there, I understand. Sold out and moved because of the droughts that had just about ruined him. Had a place in the San Pedro Valley, I think it was. Not far from Tombstone."

Hatfield nodded again. "Where's the nearest telegraph office?" he suddenly asked.

"Crater," replied the sheriff. "Railroad runs through Crater. Why?"

"I think I'll want you to send a message for me," Hatfield said. "I'll write it out in the morning. Now I think we've gabbed enough for tonight. Lead me into the cell with the least bugs and shut the door."

"Why?" asked the sheriff. "I'm not in the habit of lockin' up Rangers."

"You're going to lock this one up for tonight," Hatfield told him. "Would look sort of funny to folks if I was mavericking around after you hauled me in tonight. And by the way, bring in the Circle P bunch tomorrow and lock them up until after the coroner's jury brings in a verdict at the inquest over Curly Wilkes and those two breeds. You won't be able to hold them after the inquest, of course. No more against them than against me."

"But why get 'em on the prod any more than they are now?" the sheriff demurred.

"For a couple of reasons," Hatfield answered. "If they have clean hands, they'll cuss some but won't be overly affected for long. And making it look like you're suspicious of them might cause some other folks to get careless. That's one reason. The second? There's an old saying, 'Out of wine comes truth.' And a jigger who's good

111

and mad about something is in the same mental category as a gent who's well likkered up. He's apt to say things he wouldn't say otherwise. Somebody might do a little talking out of turn. You see, Raines, we have no definite suspect, so we have to suspect everybody for a while, until somebody tips his hand."

"Guess you're right," agreed the sheriff. "Okay, take the end cell. Hipless snoozes in there sometimes, and I reckon you won't catch anything worse than the itch from him."

15

Sheriff Raines was good as his word. About noon the following day a wrathful Circle P bunch, including Whetsall and Hang Soon, joined Hatfield in durance vile.

Brant Preston and his men spoke their opinion of the Sheriff in no uncertain terms. Hang Soon rolled apprehensive slant eyes and said things that would have tangled up a sidewinder with the colic. Hatfield vociferously demanded something to eat.

Food was brought in due time, surprisingly good and in large quantities. After getting on the outside of it, the prisoners were in a better temper.

"Just take it easy," Hatfield counselled the others. "The jury won't hold us any longer than it takes us to tell our stories. It's just a matter of form. Raines couldn't very well do anything else."

"He won't be satisfied till he gets me shot or hung," growled Preston. "He's always believed that I ran off and left Tom Garrett down in Mexico, without trying to help him. He and Garrett are brothers-in-law. Oh, well, I reckon I shouldn't hold it against him for feeling that way, but it's mighty hard to be blamed for something you didn't do."

"If you hadn't gone all out for that darned little red-headed niece of his and tried to use her dad as a —" began the irascible Crowley. Preston interrupted him with explosive violence.

"Shut your blamed mouth!" he blazed. "You're always talking out of turn!"

There was a mad glitter in his blue eyes as he spoke. Crowley flinched away from his furious glare and subsided, muttering sullenly to himself. Hatfield would have given much to have had him finish his interrupted remark.

Old Doc Beard opened court in Flintlock Finnegan's saloon shortly after midday. The news had gotten about and the big room was crowded. Jim saw *Don* Fernando Cartina who nodded to him cordially. He saw nothing of *Don* Fernando's evil appearing range boss, Pierce Kimble. Lonnie Garrett was there and she stared at him coldly.

"Guess the little lady doesn't approve of the company I'm keeping," Hatfield told himself with a rueful grin.

Last in the line of prisoners was Hang Soon. As he entered, an indignant feminine voice with a decidedly Hibernian accent exclaimed from a back seat —

"Arragh! and there's afther bein' the yaller haythen what bediviled me poor husband and led him in evil ways. Just let me get me grippers on his skinny neck and they won't be afther needin' a rope!"

Hang Soon gave a despairing squeak and tried to bolt, but was stopped by Hipless Harley.

"Me go back jail!" chattered Hang. "Me throw me 'way with key! That wife without Boss! Me wanta be allee same China!"

"You'll get a good start in that direction if you don't stop tryin' to get past me," Hipless told him grimly. "You'll get down three, four feet, anyhow."

"Two feet plenty, if get change to use um!" wailed Hang.

"Order in the court!" bawled old Doc Beard, his white whiskers bristling. "I'm runnin' this shindig and when I need any assistance I'll ask for it!"

He banged on the table with an ancient horse pistol with a muzzle the size of a nail keg. The old cannon was at full cock and several gentlemen hurriedly vacated front seats.

The jury was sworn in and the trial proceeded swiftly. After Hank Hilton had told the last story, old Doc glared venomously at the prisoners and addressed the jury.

"These hellions stick t'gether," he said, "and we ain't got no way to contradict 'em. Also, so far as we can find out, there wasn't nobody plugged but one of their own gang and two mighty mean lookin' breeds. So, gents, I calculate the only thing we can do is turn 'em loose till next time. Maybe by then the law of averages and general cussedness will thin 'em out some more. Finnegan, you will serve the court and the jury free drinks. The prisoners and the spectators'll pay for their own."

Crowley, Hilton and Kearns began celebrating their release with some cronies at one end of the bar.

Sheriff Raines was riding to Crater, in his pocket a long and carefully worded message addressed to Captain Bill McDowell, Ranger Post headquarters.

"Have the reply come to you," Hatfield directed. "You should get it within a few days. Captain Bill works fast. We may be able to get the lowdown on a couple of gents which would help a lot."

"That's right," agreed the sheriff. "Cartina and Preston both spent time in Arizona and Preston's bunch was with him. If there was anything off-color about 'em over there, the Arizona Rangers should be able to dig it out."

"Yes," nodded Hatfield. "And the warden of the penitentiary may be able to give us some information. That would be a real break. But put a flea in that telegraph operator's ear. The company rules swear him to secrecy regarding messages sent and received, but a little advice from you to keep his mouth shut won't hurt."

"He'll keep a tight latigo on his jaw after I get through talkin' to him," Sheriff Raines promised grimly.

Hatfield cast about in search of Preston but could not find him. Shortly he headed for the livery stable to see if Goldy was all right. He was in the sorrel's stall when a man and a girl paused in the doorway of the stable. Hatfield saw it was Brant Preston and Lonnie Garrett. They were conversing in low tones.

"Lonnie, I've told you time and again it wasn't my fault," Preston was saying in a weary, pleading voice. "I tried to get him out, but there wasn't a chance. I told you the story and what I said happened is just what did happen. The only thing for me to do was cut and run. I figured to circle around and go back for him, but I never had a chance. They were right on my tail until I crossed the River. You know I'm telling you the truth."

"All I know for sure," the girl replied bitterly, "is that you got away yourself and left Dad to rot in that Mexican jail. He's been there for months now. Maybe he's dead!" Her voice choked in a sob.

Preston was silent for a moment. Hatfield could see a rising glow in his darkly blue eyes. His lips twitched a little.

"Lonnie," he said abruptly, "if I risk my life going down there again and bring him back, will you do what I keep asking you to do? Will you marry me?"

The girl's face whitened. There was a hint of terror in her wide eyes.

"He won't last much longer down there," Preston said softly. "I believe I can get him out — for you. If I don't, I'll die there with him. Can I do any more? If I ride off with your promise, nothing can stop me. I'm not so terrible that marrying me would be such an awful price to pay for your dad's life."

For a long moment the girl was silent. When she spoke, it was with stiff lips, and her voice seemed to choke in her throat.

"God forgive me, Brant, I will," she said. "No!, don't touch me now. Wait — wait — until you come back — with Dad. Now please get my horse. I'll try to believe in you, Brant, even though Uncle Jed is suspicious of you."

"Jed Raines!" Preston began angrily, but his voice instantly grew gentle again. "After all, he's your dead mother's brother, and he thinks a lot of your dad, so I ain't saying anything," he finished. "I'll get your horse. Want me to ride with you?"

The girl shook her head. "No," she declined. "I promised Fernando Cartina I'd ride back with him."

Preston's eyes flashed, but he only nodded and entered the stall nearest the door. A few minutes later he led out a sturdy little pinto. The girl mounted, smiled wanly at him, and rode off, her shoulders drooping. Preston gazed after her, his lips twisting in a derisive smile. Then he shrugged his shoulders and left the stable. Hatfield rolled a cigarette and stood smoking, his eyes thoughtful. Finally he seemed to reach a decision. He reached over and rubbed Goldy's glossy neck.

"Feller," he said, "we'll be taking one whale of a chance, but I guess it's up to us to lend the little lady a hand. I believe we can pull it off. And if we do, we may be going a long way toward clearing up this mess and putting a stop to the hell that's liable to bust loose anytime. I believe it's worth trying, and we haven't anything to lose — except you and me."

Goldy snorted in what was doubtless agreement. Hatfield chuckled and went in search of Brant Preston. He found the Circle P owner in Flintlock Finnegan's place seated at a table, a bottle and glass before him. His eyes were brooding, his greeting barely civil. But Hatfield drew up a vacant chair on the other side of the table and sat down. There were men at the bar including Hank Hilton, Wes Crowley and Tart Kearns, now well on the road to a royal drunk, but the nearby tables were unoccupied. Hatfield leaned his elbows on the table and stared across at Preston. His voice was a soft drawl —

"Preston, just where is that calaboose in which you left Miss Garrett's dad?"

Brant Preston's head jerked up and his eyes were black with anger.

"So you were listenin'! Why, you —"

The Lone Wolf's quiet voice stemmed the tirade before it got under way.

"I couldn't very well keep from hearing," he said. "I was in the stall with my horse and I didn't figure it would help matters any by me walking out in the middle of your powwow. Now, tighten up your rope a minute till I'm finished. I'm not asking questions that are none of my business just to be curious. I happen to know something of Mexican jails and as I recall, Miss Garrett said her dad had been in one of them for months. If he stays there much longer, there won't be any use of him coming out except to bust up a dull day for the buzzards. You ought to know that, seeing as you say you've looked at the outside from one yourself."

Preston's eyes flickered slightly and he swallowed, as if savoring an unpleasant memory.

"Yeah, I was there, too," he admitted, "though not for long. I'll tell you how it all happened —"

He cleared his throat and began talking slowly, apparently choosing his words with care. And as he talked Jim Hatfield could envision a table in a Cuevas saloon around which sat a half dozen or so men. Preston was there and *Don* Fernando Cartina. There were also Tom Garrett, Lonnie's father, Craig Doyle, who owned the K8, and several cowboys.

"I'm sick and tired of the whole business," Garrett was swearing. "I lost another herd this week. Few more raids and I won't have enough beef on my spread to make a sandwich."

Don Fernando nodded his handsome head. "We're all catching it," he agreed. "The question is, what are we going to do?"

"I know what I'm going to do!" Garrett declared grimly.

"What's that, Tom?" asked Craig Doyle. Garrett leaned across the table and spoke impressively.

"I'm going to get my steers back, that's what," he rumbled. "How? You just listen. Everybody knows where those beefs go when they cross the river; they go to Tijerna, Juan Cheno's town."

"Yeah," agreed Preston, "they do. That's why we can't do anything about it. Cheno is a regular king down that way. Even old President Diaz can't do anything with him. Diaz is scared of him — scared Cheno may start a revolution or somethin'. Cheno ain't got no education, can't read or write, but he sure has got brains of a sort."

"Brains of a widelooper!" growled Garrett. "Well, gents, I'm going to tie a knot in *Señor* Cheno's rope. I'm going to ride right down to his *El Aguila* ranch, cut me out a herd and bring 'em back across the river. You fellers with me?"

For a moment there was stunned silence. Then young Craig Doyle let out a whoop.

"I'm with you, Tom," he declared. "If Cheno can run 'em from this side, we can run 'em from his. You in on it, Brant?"

For a moment Preston's face was uncertain. Garrett leaned forward, boring the younger man with his hot eyes.

"Fine chance you ever getting married, the way your cattle's disappearing," he remarked.

Preston flushed, his lips tightened.

"All right," he replied quickly. "I'll go with you, Tom. I can take the chance if you can."

Don Fernando Cartina leaned forward and spoke earnestly.

"You are all mad," he declared. "You are attempting the impossible. Cheno knows every move made along the border. If an armed force rides toward *El Aguila,* he will be notified. You will just end by getting killed."

"We're takin' that chance," Garrett replied grimly. "I don't blame you for not joining us. Your property is chiefly mines — cattle's just a side issue with you, but it's the whole works with the rest of us."

Two nights later Preston, Garrett, Craig Doyle, and five punchers crossed the shallow river and rode south. All night they rode and when daylight came, they holed up in a burr oak grove and slept. That night, when the moon flooded the rangeland with ghostly silver, they swiftly rode south again.

El Aguila, Cheno's vast ranch, was as large as some kingdoms. Cheno, bloated, sinister, spiderlike, ruled it like a king or feudal baron. In Tijerna, his headquarters, he had a small army of hard riding, hard shooting *vaqueros.* Another army was scattered over his many thousands of acres. Not even the grim old tyrant of Mexico City could suppress him. Diaz hated Cheno and feared him. He raided across the river and defied the Texas authorities to do anything about it.

Cattle by the thousand grazed on *El Aguila.* Tom Garrett and his companions approached one of the vast, untended herds. They cut out as many as they could drive swiftly and turned their heads north.

"Just too easy!" exulted Garrett. "Didn't I tell you we could do it!"

His men scattered about the herd, urging it on. On either side brooded dark hills, mysterious in the moonlight. The valley through which they were passing narrowed.

From those silent hills suddenly burst a stormblast of death. Rifles spurted red from the shelter of rock and tree trunk. Sixguns rattled as Cheno's yelling *vaqueros* swept down upon the doomed band.

Craig Doyle died at the first volley. Three of the cowboys died also. The two others and Garrett went down fighting, the punchers riddled with bullets, Garrett with a creased skull. A rope sailed through the air and settled over Brant Preston's shoulders. In a moment he was helpless, bound by turn on turn of rawhide. He and Garrett were thrown across horses. Their captors headed for Tijerna.

Cheno the merciless grinned at them and licked his thick lips.

"You will remain as my guests, *caballeros*," he purred. "For long you will remain."

He waved a fat hand and the prisoners were hustled away and thrown into the filthy little calaboose that crouched on the banks of a sluggish creek that skirted Cheno's town. Garrett was weak and sick, his head badly gashed. Preston was unhurt.

Days passed during which Garrett regained some measure of his strength. They plotted escape. Hour after hour Preston whittled and shaped a piece of wood with a knife he had managed to smuggle in. One evening when the grim jailer shoved their scanty meal through the bars, he looked up and stared into the black muzzle of what appeared to be a serviceable gun. Preston's cold voice bit at him —

"Open that door or have your brains spattered over the wall!"

Gasping and trembling, the jailer obeyed. The two prisoners slipped out, bound and gagged the jailer and threw him into the cell. Preston tossed aside the wooden gun and replaced it with the jailer's big Smith & Wesson. Then they crept through the shadows toward a stable in which were housed the mounts of some of Cheno's "soldiers."

"*Quien es?*" asked the wrangler as they loomed in the dark doorway. Garrett leaped like a panther and smashed him between the eyes with his fist. Working at frantic speed, they saddled two horses, mounted and rode through the low doorway — straight into a troop of Cheno's *vaqueros!*

Bending low in the saddle, lashing his horse, Preston burst through their ranks before the surprised Mexicans knew what was going on. Close after him thundered Garrett. Guns boomed behind them. The *vaqueros* gave chase.

Preston, on the better horse, forged ahead. Suddenly he heard a yell, then a howl of triumph. Garrett's horse was down and Garrett lay senseless beside him in the dust. For a moment

Preston hesitated, pulling his bronk to a sliding halt, but before he could turn the *vaqueros* were swarming about Garrett. Preston whirled his mount and hightailed for the Border.

"Maybe I ought to have gone back for him, anyhow, and died there," Preston concluded, staring into the Ranger's face, "but right then I couldn't figure that it would do either of us any good. I calculated if I could get across the river I might be able to do Tom some good from this side. I've tried, damn hard, but so far I ain't been able to accomplish anything. I did find out he was still alive and in jail."

"Yes, Cheno is the sort that knows it's tougher being shut up in that hell-hole than being dead," Hatfield nodded.

"I had to tell Lonnie about it," Preston went on. "She sort of held it against me and folks hereabouts didn't think any too well of the whole business. They seem to figure we just went on a widelooping trip. What bothers me most is to think of Garrett there in that rotten jail."

He stopped speaking, and sat brooding into his glass.

Hatfield also sat silent for some minutes, his mind working swiftly. Preston's story had been told in a straightforward manner, but there were certain points the Lone Wolf felt could possibly be questioned. In the fight with the *vaqueros,* everybody had been shot but Preston. He had merely been lassoed, which was very considerate on the part of the *vaqueros.* Next a hardboiled jailer had been fooled by the old wooden gun trick. Then a company of *vaqueros* had been conveniently stationed outside the jail at just the right time. Garrett was recaptured, while Preston got away. Perhaps everything happened just as Preston said, but singular coincidence appeared to play a strong part in the proceeding. Preston might be telling the whole truth, but he had certainly gotten the breaks.

Hatfield voiced the plan he had evolved.

"So it bothers you that Garrett is in Cheno's jail," he remarked. "Well, why leave him there?"

"Uh-huh, why?" Preston mimicked. "How in Hades am I going to keep from leaving him there, that's what I'm trying to figure."

Hatfield's steady eyes never left the other's face. "You can keep from it by getting him out and bringing him home as you promised Miss Garrett you'd do," he said.

Preston swore viciously. "Yes, I know I promised, and God knows I want to keep the promise," he replied, "but how? Cheno's got five hundred men in that town of his and five hundred more scattered around his spreads. How am I going to buck a young army?"

The Lone Wolf's voice snapped at him like a pistol shot —

"By using what I think you've got — brains! That is, if you've got the guts to go along with them."

Preston's face turned livid and his eyes seemed to blaze blue fire under the searing contempt in the Ranger's voice. He swallowed convulsively, steadied his own voice with a visible effort.

"Feller," he said, "I'm not used to being talked to this way, but I'll listen to what you've got to suggest."

Hatfield hauled the makin's from his pocket and rolled a cigarette before replying.

"I know Cheno's got a small army of his owlhoots down there," he said after the brain tablet was going good. "And I know we haven't got the men to go up against him, but a snake can crawl through a hole that a grizzly can't — and can do plenty of damage after he gets through. Now if about three men — say you and I and Crowley — were to slip down there disguised as Mexicans or breeds and do a little snooping around, maybe we could find a way to put one over on *Señor* Cheno."

Preston digested the Ranger's suggestion. "All you need is a dirty blanket and a *sombrero* to make Crowley a Mexican," he agreed. "And all I need is a little grease and some velvet pants to get by. I've got Spanish blood, you know. My mother's people, one generation removed, were Mexican-Spanish. But you, feller, there's no turning you into a Mexican, I'm afraid."

"You're right about that," Hatfield conceded, "but I know how to make up to pass for an Indian. All I need is buckskin pants, a shirt, and a chance to use a kettle in the ranchhouse kitchen once I've collected a few herbs and berries that aren't hard to come by in this section. Posing as, say, a Comanche, I wouldn't need to know much Spanish either."

He deliberately refrained from confiding in Preston that he could speak the language with extraordinary fluency.

Preston considered. Hatfield could sense thoughts rising in his mind like unseen things floating upward through murky water. Suddenly he seemed to come to a decision. His thin lips tightened a little and there was a glow in his eyes.

"Hatfield," he said, "I'm going to take a chance. It's more than likely we'll all three of us end up getting cashed in or keeping old Tom company in that calaboose, but I'm with you. I can answer for Crowley, too. That little hellion is in for anything that promises a fight. I'll get hold of him, sober him up and haul him back to the ranchhouse. Will you take care of the clothes and things we need? There's a general store down the street where you should be able to get every-thing. Here's money. No, you've got to take it. I'm footing the bills this chore. You've done your part figuring it out. Perhaps you'd better stay in town over night and take care of things in the morning. I'll take Crowley back to the spread to-night before he gets started on a regular gulley-washer."

"Okay," Hatfield agreed. "I'll need daylight anyway to hunt out the stuff I need for the dye. And by the way, Preston, I'd suggest you don't talk to anybody about what we've got in mind. Not to anybody. If there's a slip-up of some kind, we'll have a reception committee waiting for us when we hit Cheno's town and we won't enjoy the festivities."

"You're blamed right we won't," Preston growled agreement. "End up spread-eagled over an ant heap, like as not. Well, so long. I'll round up Crowley and get going."

Crowley was a good deal more than half drunk, but Preston managed to haul him away from Flintlock's bar and get him headed for the ranch. Hatfield watched them ride out of town, a speculative look in his eyes. Preston had seemed quite anxious to part company with him, which was of interest, the Lone Wolf thought.

The following morning, Hatfield had no trouble obtaining the needed articles from the general store. After completing his purchases, he dropped in at the sheriff's office.

"Is there a gunsmith in this town?" he asked Raines.

"Old Si Releford repairs busted shootin' irons along with other things," replied Raines.

"Can he be trusted to keep his mouth shut?"

"Huh!" snorted the sheriff. "That old pelican doesn't even talk to himself. He keeps a tight latigo on his jaw if anybody ever did. You can trust him. His shop is three doors down from Flintlock's place."

Hatfield nodded, said goodbye to the sheriff and left the office. He found Releford's little shop without difficulty. He decided the sheriff was right in his estimate of the cantankerous little gnome of a man who regarded him belligerently when he stepped in the door. He did not hesitate to show his star, cautioning the shopkeeper not to talk. Releford's reply was a noncommittal grunt. He cocked a birdlike eye at the Ranger.

"Okay, okay," he said in a voice that was almost frightening, so awesomely deep and rumbling it was. "Okay, go ahead, I know what you come for."

"For what?" Hatfield asked.

"To ask questions," Releford replied. "That's what your sort always comes in here for."

Hatfield hid his amusement with difficulty. "Okay," he said. "Has anybody brought in a rifle with a busted firing pin of late?"

"Uh-huh," replied Releford. "About an hour back."

Hatfield's eyes glowed. "Who was it?" he asked.

"I don't know who the blazes he was," answered Releford. "A Mexican-breed, I'd say. One of Fernando Cartina's hands, the chances are. Cartina hires *vaqueros*. I don't recollect ever seein' him before, but those breeds all look alike."

"Is he coming back for the saddle gun?"

"Nope," said Releford. "He waited and took it with him. Wasn't much of a chore. Last I saw of him he was ridin' north out of town."

Hatfield suppressed his disappointment and was silent for a moment. Then he asked a question to corroborate his own conclusions —

"The circular edge of the head of a brand-new firing pin would be clean cut and sharp, wouldn't it?"

"You could cut your finger on it."

"How long would it remain that way?"

"A dozen shots would start to burr over the edge," said Releford.

Hatfield nodded. "Thanks, old-timer," he said.

"Don't mention it," said Releford. "Come in again when you want to know something."

Hatfield chuckled and left the shop. "Blazes!" he exploded disgustedly when he reached the street. "Missed what might have been a promising lead by an hour! Well, maybe some time I'll get a break. So the jigger rode north? A mile outside of town and he could turn in any direction. I'm right back where I started."

Several times in the course of the ride back to the ranch, Hatfield dismounted to gather a handful of berries, a few leaves or a root or two from a soft hillside. These he carefully wrapped in a handkerchief and carried along with him. At the ranchhouse kitchen the whole mess went into a small iron pot and simmered over a slow fire, much to the disgust of Hang Soon.

"Smell like dead cow inside buzzard's belly," declared the Chinaman. "Me hang nose on line with clothes pin — allee same shut tight on outside."

Hatfield grinned and set the contents of the pot aside to cool. When he could bear the touch of it he smeared the thick liquid over his face, neck, hands and forearms. The result was startling. With his skin now stained to a reddish bronze, his hawk nose, high cheek bones and straight black hair, the resemblance to a Plains Indian chief would have fooled a Black Foot or a Sioux. A suit of frayed buckskin which he had managed to pick up in the Cuevas store made the disguise complete.

"Me gonna take hair off and put um in pocket," declared Hang. "No want um hang on belt."

"Don't worry, Hang, you're not going to get scalped," chuckled a villainous looking little "Mexican" who lounged in the door, a corn husk cigarette drooping from his lower lip.

"Mist' Jim look bad, Mist' Crowley, you look from worse," declared Hang. "Mist' Preston look bad from worse of all!"

Crowley and Preston *were* a forbidding pair, Hatfield was forced to admit. His black brows drew together as he gazed at the latter, garbed in Mexican attire, *sombrero* pulled low over his smouldering eyes. *Once again he recalled a vision of a dark, sinister face rushing toward him out of the night.*

The bonfire stars of Texas burned golden over their heads, the blue dust of the dusk deepened to black velvet about them, as three ominous figures crossed the murmuring flood of the Rio Grande and rode into that brooding, mysterious land beyond.

16

It was mid-afternoon, with Tijerna lying sun-drenched and shiftless at the foot of a towering mountain whose crest of naked rock seemed to rake the brassy-blue sky. Forests of scrub oak and piñon pine, like cool green and blue shadows, clothed the sides and shoulders of the old giant, but the needle spire that fanged up like a blackened tooth in a rotting jawbone was un-draped save for the saffron waves of light that streamed about it. As Hatfield and his two companions rode into Tijerna, those waves were turning from saffron to rose with little trickles of crimson spilling down the grooved crags like pulses of slow blood. Tijerna itself, with its straggle of adobes sprawling toward the mountain, its *cantinas,* gambling halls and pleasure palaces, was splashed with molten gold. Over everything hung a powdering of yellow dust. Even the *serapes* and *sombreros* of the loungers about the plaza were thick with it. Dogs wallowed in it as well as hogs and naked children. Scrawny chickens flapped up small clouds with indolent wings as they burrowed out little hollows. The hoofs of the newcomers' horses plumped in it with soft little "chucks." Goldy sneezed and rolled his eyes in disgust.

Hatfield, his red-bronze face devoid of expression, thought that never before had he encountered such vicious shiftlessness as Cheno's town evinced. Beady eyes glinted sideways to watch their progress along the street. No word was said, the dark faces of the loungers told nothing of what was going on in their furtive minds, but the Ranger could sense an air of intense calculation and dangerous curiosity. He wondered if those snaky eyes could penetrate their disguises. If such were the case, he knew that they had not one chance in a thousand of getting out of the town alive. Every man he saw was armed, and he knew that every man in the town was one of Cheno's bandit-soldiers who, despite their appearance of utter indolence, were vicious, alert fighters who knew nothing of either fear or mercy. These men were one with the three hard-faced Yaqui-Mexicans he had encountered on the banks of the little stream as he rode to Cuevas. They were kin, also, to the men who had tried so desperately to murder him in the Cuevas saloon and later in the Circle P bunkhouse. His opinion of what was back of the seemingly senseless killings and torturings that had terrorized the bloody triangle north of the Rio Grande was strengthened.

"*El Hombre*," he muttered under his breath. "*El Hombre* — Juan Cheno! Wonder if the two do tie up. If they do — if they're the same! Hell —"

His black brows drew together as he visioned what it would mean to the border country if Cheno, the bandit, the revolutionary, really was the dread and mysterious *El Hombre,* the very mention of whom caused the *peons* of the river villages to blanch and shiver.

"Well figure on that later," he decided as they drew up in front of a tawdry *meson* — the kind of tavern that catered to trade such as he and his ragged and dirty companions represented.

They entered the inn, Preston and Crowley conversing glumly in liquidly slurred Spanish, asked for food for themselves and provender for their horses. The innkeeper demanded payment in advance and Hatfield handed out the required amount in small silver coins. The innkeeper, who acted as his own wrangler, eyed the big sorrel greedily, turned and found the cold eyes of the "Indian" owner of the animal staring down into his face. The "Indian" said nothing, only he drew, from somewhere, an enormous knife and ran a bronzed finger tip along the razor-sharp edge, meanwhile gazing hungrily at the man's shock of greasy black hair. The other turned a dirty gray under the dirt that encrusted his swarthy face.

"*Señor,* your *caballo* will receive such care as I would lavish on my eldest son, had I a son," he exclaimed. "Fear not — he will be at your call, instantly and at all times."

The "Indian" said nothing. He put the knife away with evident reluctance and stalked into the eating room of the inn with the gait of a mountain lion.

"*Madre de Dios!*" breathed the innkeeper as he

shuffled toward the stable.

Preston and Crowley were hard put to hide the grins that twitched their lips.

"I got a hunch we ain't gonna be bothered by hoss thieves," breathed the latter.

They ate hugely of a stew of black beans and meat, fiery with ground red peppers, and flat *tortilla* biscuits, washing it all down with *pulque*. The Mexican beer, brewed from cactus juice, was heady and good. The food, although coarse, was also good and well prepared.

"We're bein' watched, mighty close," Hatfield told his companions between mouthfuls. "They're a suspicious lot here — reckon they got plenty reason to be. I got a hunch somebody'll be drifting in to sound us out before long. Cheno doesn't let strangers ride into his town without finding out something about them. Brant, you do the talking."

They had just ordered another drink when a slim young Mexican in velvet jacket and pantaloons sauntered through the door and with a glance around the room, strolled over to their table.

"Pardon, *caballeros*," he said courteously, "but I could not but notice the wonderful *caballo* ridden by the tall *señor*. I am a lover of fine horses and I hope you will not consider it an affront when I say that I would greatly like to purchase the animal. It is for sale, perhaps, if the price is right, *Si?*"

Hatfield vigorously shook his head but said

nothing. Preston took up the conversation in Spanish.

"The Chief thinks greatly of his horse," he explained. "Men died when he acquired it."

The other raised his delicate eyebrows. "*Si*, I understand," he replied, instantly accepting the implication that the horse was stolen.

"You have ridden far?" he asked

"From the River, and beyond," replied Preston.

Again the other nodded. The implication there was that the big horse, and probably the others as well, had been stolen from a Texas ranch.

"You will drink with us, *señor?*" invited Preston. This time he paid for the drinks with a gold piece which did not escape the guest's keen eyes. Neither did the glint of more gold in Preston's palm. He was beginning to understand better why these three had ridden from beyond the River.

"You will remain in our town for some days?" he asked.

"Perhaps," replied Preston. "*Quien sabe!*" with a shrug. A moment later he asked with elaborate casualness a question apparently irrelevant to the conversation —

"The *rurales*, they come here often?" He knew very well that *El Presidente's* mounted police never visited Cheno's town nor rode over his millions of acres. The other knew very well that he knew it and grinned his appreciation. His voice was cordial and comradely when he replied.

"No one in the town of *El Gran General* need fear the *rurales*," he stated, voicing the title given Cheno by his followers.

Preston returned the grin. Crowley grinned also and Hatfield gave vent to a guttural grunt that might have signified pleasure or any other emotion. After another drink the stranger bade them a courteous *"buenos dias"* and left the room.

"Well, that's that," said Hatfield. "He's got us down as a gang of raiders with the Border too hot to hold us. Another day or two and chances are we'll get an invitation to join Cheno's army. Now the first thing is to get in touch with Garrett. Crowley, I calculate that'll be your chore. You ought to be able to mix best with the rooster fighters and gamblers and such. Garrett's got to know what we're going to do before we start anything. Now here's what I have in mind —"

He spoke rapidly for some minutes and as he went on, Crowley's little eyes snapped and he chuckled with pleasure.

"Feller, you're good!" he declared. "I been wondering all along how in Sam Hill we were going to bust open that jail without dynamite or somethin'. If that scheme don't work, I'm a sheepherder. Don't worry, I'll get word to old Tom; he'll be ready and waiting."

Crowley set out on his chore the following morning. Hatfield remained with Preston whose side he never left for an instant. He might as well have been the ranchowner's shadow on a sunny day. If Preston noticed this, he did not intimate so by word or gesture.

It took Crowley less than twenty-four hours to make good his word.

"One of the fellers I been gambling with had a bunky that sliced another hellion over a cock fight," he explained. "Cheno had him locked up a while to cool off. Him and Tom are the only prisoners in the jail right now. They ain't locked in no cells, day or night — ain't no cells in that hog-waller, that's why — just one big room with a door opening into another room where the jailer sleeps. The one window, barred good and strong, looks over the creek that runs behind the jail just as you figured, Jim. The back of the jail is set on high posts because the creek gets up a bit when it rains hard. Water is washing against those posts right now. I told Tom to be ready to-night."

"Time for us to move, then," Jim told the others.

An hour later they were riding south out of the town. The inhabitants watched them depart with expressionless, beady eyes but offered no objection. They were among the lonely hills before sundown. They made camp in a little clearing, cooked some food and allowed the horses to graze and roll. When twilight spread its golden-purple mantle across the rolling rangeland, they saddled up and headed back for Tijerna, letting the horses take it easy. It was past midnight when they pulled up on the far bank of the shallow creek, directly opposite the little jail. Preston led a spare horse they had managed to cut out of a string grazing near a lonely ranchhouse a few miles south of Tijerna.

Leaving Crowley to hold the horses, Jim and Preston waded noiselessly across trailing three stout ropes behind them. They paused under the window in the black shadow of the building and listened. Wading the river in the pale shimmer of the starlight had been a ticklish business and each heaved a sigh of relief when the profound gloom of the shadow swallowed them up. As they strained their ears, a sound made itself evident, a rhythmic rumble that rose and fell without cessation. Suddenly it was punctuated by an explosive snort, then once again it resumed the unbroken tenor of its way.

"Ha!" breathed Hatfield with a barely audible chuckle, "it's just the jailer snoring. Let him snore. He couldn't do anything to suit me better right now. All right, feller, up you go."

He seized Preston about the thighs and without the least apparent effort hoisted him until his wet boots rested on the Ranger's sinewy shoulders.

"Old Tom's waitin' at the window," Preston breathed down to him, "the other feller's asleep. All right, pass me up the ropes."

Hatfield handed the wet lines to him one by one and Preston tied them securely to the stout window bars which were set deep in a heavy wooden frame. When the last was knotted tight,

140

Hatfield eased the ranchowner back into the water. Silently as before, they crept back across the river, Hatfield's flesh crawling as the starlight revealed them plainly to any chance watcher. He momentarily expected a yell of alarm and the blast of a rifle. Little Crowley swore relief as they climbed dripping up the bank.

"All right," Hatfield told him as they mounted. "All together now, not too fast — don't want to make a bronc change ends. A good jerk at first, then a steady pull till the bars tear loose. That wood isn't going to hold against three good cutting horses. Let's go!"

The ropes tightened with a hum like giant harp strings as the three big horses straightened them out and dug in their hoofs. Across the river there was a snapping and creaking sound.

"She's comin'!" panted Jim. "Go to it, Goldy horse! Give 'em hell, feller!"

The giant sorrel snorted like a steam engine and gave a mighty lunge. From the direction of the jail sounded a rending crash. It was followed by a prodigious splintering and crackling, a tremendous splash and a piercing yell muffled by thick walls.

The splash subsided to a series of gurgling ripples, but the yells continued, gaining volume with every volley. There was also a sound of thrashing, thudding and wallowing, and gasping curses in Spanish and English!

"Good gosh-all-hemlock!" bawled Crowley.

"The pull was too damn much for that under-pinning in back of the calaboose. It busted loose and dumped the whole contraption into the creek. Listen to that Mex jailer yell — his room is in the water and the door's on the side that's against the bottom. Good thing for him the water ain't deep!"

"Good thing for us the door is on the bottom!" growled Preston. "What's all that hell-a-fallutin' going on inside the calaboose? Sounds like a passel of wildcats havin' a free-for all!"

"It's one Texan and one Mexican having a free-for-all!" Hatfield told him. "Tom Garrett and that Mexican gambler are having a little party all their own. Wonder which head's coming out the window first?"

"I know which one better come out first!" replied Preston grimly, slipping his rifle from the boot.

"Something better happen damn quick!" bawled Crowley, hopping in his saddle with apprehension. "The whole town's woke up — listen to 'em yell."

From inside the capsized jail sounded a hollowy and watery boom.

"Jailer's got a shotgun goin'!" Preston grated.

"What the Sam Hill's he shooting at, fish?" demanded Crowley.

"You'll soon find out if he manages to get that door open," Jim replied. "Wait! Those fellers on the bank over there aren't shooting at fish! Let 'em have it — they've spotted us!"

Bright flashes were rippling along the far bank of the creek. Rifles and six-guns crackled. Bullets whined about the trio on horseback. Almost before the first slug had screeched past, they were on the ground, their rifles blazing defiance to Cheno's "soldiers." Yells and shrieks went up as bullets found their mark. There was a rush of dark figures up the bank for cover. Hatfield strained his ears for the sound he most feared — the click of galloping hoofs.

"Somebody's coming out of the jail!" bawled Preston, flinging up his rifle. He held a steady bead on the shadowy figure emerging from the splintered window, his eyes glowing hotly back of the sights.

"Blinkin' blazes!" he exploded. "The sidewinder's done for Tom! Garrett ain't got no whiskers!"

His fingers squeezed the trigger. Crowley let out a yell of warning!

17

Barely in time, Hatfield's hand streaked out and knocked the rifle up, the bullet whined toward the stars and Preston cursed like a madman. Hatfield's hair-trigger mind had interpreted the significance of Crowley's yell. He wrested the rifle from the ranchowner before he could direct a second shot at the form squirming madly through the narrow opening.

"Garrett's grown whiskers since he was locked up!" he roared in explanation.

"I'd forgot to tell you about it!" chattered Crowley between flinging shots across the creek. "God, that was close!"

Preston's face was contorted, but he only mumbled curses. Hatfield thrust his own loaded rifle into his hands and began shoving cartridges into Preston's Winchester. His slim, sensitive fingers caressed the firing mechanism as he flung the rifle to his shoulder. In the depths of his green eyes were little crawling fires.

Garrett was in the water now and foaming through it toward the bank. Bullets kicked up splashes and geysers all around him, but the withering fire of the three deadly rifles gave the Mexicans too much to think about to permit careful aim. In a few seconds Garrett came clawing up the bank, water dripping from his scraggly gray beard and his long hair. Hatfield yelled directions and he flung himself onto the spare horse whose saddle consisted of a blanket roped to its bony back. The others mounted in haste, still firing. Above the uproar could be heard the jailer's frenzied bawls and the reports of his shotgun as he tried to blast a way out of his water prison.

Hatfield also heard another sound — the sound he dreaded. Horses were racing toward the creek bank. Even as rescuers and rescued got under way, a troop of Cheno's irregular cavalry stormed into the water.

"Ride," the Ranger barked. "Never mind any more shootin'. We got to outrun them."

Ride they did through the pale shimmer of the starlight, heading for that far distant River to the north that spelled safety. The false dawn fled across the sky and the black hour that follows it closed down. Still they pounded on and still their pursuers held grimly on their trail while the "borrowed" horse that Tom Garrett rode was beginning to falter.

Hatfield glanced anxiously behind. He could see the pursuit, irregular dark blotches on the faintly glowing prairie. To his left, looming gigantic against the darkling sky, was a range of wild hills. He had noticed those hills on the way into Mexico and knew they were gashed by canyons and gorges. With a word to the others, he slanted his speeding horse to the left.

"If we get in those hills we'll get lost sure as

lightnin'," protested Crowley.

"And if we don't, we're going to find ourselves *in* blazes in less than an hour," the Ranger told him grimly. "It's our only chance to shake them off. They'll lose sight of us in those canyons and they'll be scared to come riding hell-bent-for-election after us and risk a drygulching."

Hatfield knew what the others did not — that it was the slower speed of their horses, particularly the one Garrett rode, that allowed the pursuers to continue their slow gain. Goldy could walk away from Cheno's riders as if their bronks were standing still. But the Ranger gave that no consideration. His speed depended on the slowest horse of the four, for so long as one of his companions remained on the wrong side of the Rio Grande, there too the Lone Wolf would be battling grimly. Swift minutes passed and the black mouth of a canyon swallowed them up. On they sped at breakneck speed, risking a fall that would be fatal at every stride the gasping horses took. The canyon twisted through the hills like a snake through a cactus patch. The mouth of a side canyon yawned a darker blotch in the shadowy wall. Hatfield unhesitatingly turned into it. A little farther on he led the way into still another narrow gorge whose close-set walls flung back the echo of their horses' hoofs with a sound like rolling rifle fire. The rosy glow of the true dawn was stealing across the sky when at last he called a halt on the banks of a brawling little stream that foamed from a narrow cleft in

146

the gorge wall and plunged into another on the far side. While the horses drank and caught their wind, he slipped back down the canyon and listened intently. There was no sign of the pursuit.

"Calculate we've lost them," he muttered thankfully. "Likewise, I figure we've lost ourselves plumb proper."

They crossed the stream and rode on up the canyon for another hour. They had food enough in their saddlebags for a couple of meals and where an abrupt narrowing of the canyon walls made surprise by the pursuers almost impossible, they stopped and ate. Over the crude breakfast, Hatfield talked with Garrett.

The rancher was not so old as he had at first surmised. His scraggly beard was streaked with gray, but there was none showing in his tawny hair. The resemblance between him and his daughter was striking. Hatfield liked his brief word of thanks to all concerned in his rescue and his dismissal of the subject from then on.

"That jigger in the jail with me tried to keep me from getting out," he said in explaining the row that was kicked up after the building tumbled into the water. "I got a notion he was planted there by Cheno to keep an eye on me. There were several of them in there during the past six months, all of them on some funny sounding charge. Soon as one would go out, another would come in. There were other fellers there, too, every now and then, but they didn't stay long. Pretty soon they were taken out and I'd hear rifles going off. They'd never come back. Calculate they were stood up against a wall and blown loose from themselves. That was Cheno's way of getting rid of fellers that were in his way."

He paused, puffing hungrily on the cigarette Hatfield had rolled for him.

"I heard some funny things from those fellers while I was in there," he added. "There's blue blazes gettin' ready to bust loose in this section or I'm much mistaken. There's a real uprising against *El Presidente* in the making — one that's being managed proper and with a big man back of it. Money for it's been pouring down from our side the Rio Grande. Just where it's coming from I couldn't find out, but there's plenty of it. Cheno's getting a real army together, too. Those *soldados* in Tijerna are nothing compared to what he's got back in the hills. I heard there was another army being got together and drilled someplace else — don't know where, but it's a good one and armed proper with new rifles."

"I didn't calculate Cheno had the brains or get-up to pull any deal like that," pondered Preston. Garrett grunted scornfully.

"He hasn't," declared the owner of the Bowtie ranch "The feller back of all this is some really big and brainy jigger. Don't seem anybody knows his name. They call him —"

Jim Hatfield, who had been listening intently to Garrett's story suddenly tensed, eyes narrowing, muscles rippling along his lean bronzed jaw. His mouth tightened like a bear trap and his strangely colored eyes were cold as the sky of a rainy dawn as Garrett repeated his last remark —

"Yeah, funny thing to call him, ain't it? But that's what they call him, just *El Hombre, The Man!*"

18

As they rode on through the morning sunlight, Jim Hatfield was silent and thoughtful. Many things that had puzzled him were clear now, but the solution of the mystery was not yet apparent, nor was he yet certain who was the man behind the outrages that had terrorized the bloody triangle. He had certain suspicions, but no proof that would stand up under the test. The death mask face of Pierce Kimble swam like an evil vision before his eyes, but so far there was nothing to connect the F Bar C foreman with any unlawful act.

"That jigger *may* have more brains than he looks to have," he mused thoughtfully. "Well, I sure haven't much to go on — a busted rifle cartridge and a little red dust, but a jigger can trip over a busted shell, and enough dust is the makings of a grave. Well, we'll let all that pass for a spell; right now the big thing is to get out of this section that the devil forgot to shovel down below. It's not going to be easy."

It wasn't. Fully three days passed before half starved and haggard with fatigue and lack of sleep, they sloshed through the shallow waters of the Rio Grande and thankfully landed on Texas soil. Garrett rode to the Circle P with them for clean clothes and a shave.

In the course of the ride, Hatfield had gotten an opportunity to talk with Garrett alone. The Bowtie owner's account of what happened on the night of the fateful raid into Mexico and afterward dovetailed perfectly with Preston's story as told to Hatfield in the Cuevas saloon.

"But it doesn't clear up the points I considered questionable," he told himself. "That doesn't mean overly much, though. I'm getting exactly nowhere fast."

They found Tart Kearns and Hilton in the ranchhouse with Hang Soon. Tart's usually good natured face was set in hard lines.

"By Gawd, it's time you got back," was his greeting. "Hello, Tom, where in Sam Hill did *you* come from? How'd you get out of the calaboose?"

"What's the matter, Tart?" asked Brant Preston. "Where's Whetsall?"

"Dead," Kearns returned grimly.

"Dead! Why, what the — what happened? How —"

"Pierce Kimble shot him between the eyes," replied Kearns.

"What!"

"Uh-huh, drilled him dead center."

Preston opened his mouth to shoot a barrage of questions. Jim Hatfield's cool tones stopped him.

"Suppose," suggested the Ranger, "we let Tart start at the beginning and tell us what happened." Preston nodded silently.

"It was like this," began Kearns. "Me and Whetsall were in Flintlock's place drinking together. Whetsall started across the room for the lunch counter to glom onto a sandwich. You know how the counter is arranged — along the wall to the left of the door. Whetsall was right opposite the door when Pierce Kimble came in. Whetsall saw him and stopped dead still. Pierce stopped, too, and they looked at each other. Then Whetsall said something, I couldn't catch what, and went for his gun. Pierce didn't move till the old jigger had cleared leather. Then he pulled, that funny double cross-pull of his, and shot right and left before Whetsall could squeeze his trigger. Whetsall got both slugs right between the eyes where Kimble always plants 'em. He was dead when he hit the floor."

"Self defense again!" Preston exclaimed bitterly.

"Sure, guess you have to call it that," agreed Kearns. "If Kimble hadn't pulled, Whetsall would have drilled him all right. But it was a plain, cold-blooded killing just the same. The old feller never had a chance. Nobody ever has a chance against that infernal double cross-pull of Kimble's. I never saw anybody wear double holster guns with the butts to the front before, and I never saw anybody could pull 'em like Kimble does. God! but he's fast! You couldn't see his hand move!"

"And pulled 'em both across?" Hatfield asked. "That is a plumb out of the ordinary draw." In his eyes was a sudden leaping light, on his face the expression of a man who has suddenly solved a bland, elusive problem.

"I was mad as a rattler," went on Kearns, "but I did have sense enough not to brace Kimble. Otherwise I wouldn't be here telling you about it."

"What did Kimble do?" asked Preston

"Went to the sheriff's office and gave himself up like he always does," snorted Kearns. "They'll hold an inquest tomorrow morning and he'll be turned loose like he always is. Twenty men saw Whetsall reach first."

Preston swore viciously. "I've a notion to go to town and brace that corpse-faced killer!" he declared.

Tart Kearns laughed derisively. "You trying to be funny?" he asked. "You're pretty slick, and I'm not denying it, but you'd have about as much chance against Pierce Kimble as a rabbit in a hounddog's mouth. He'd make you look like a snail climbing a greased log, and you know it."

Preston swore. "You're right," he admitted. "But I hope I don't run into Kimble tomorrow after the inquest. If he begins throwing the kind of talk at me he's capable of, I may not be able to hold back. I've got to go, though, and try and find out if poor Whetsall has any kin folks and arrange for having him planted."

"Brant," Hatfield said, "why don't you let me go in? Kimble hardly knows me and wouldn't be likely to be on the prod against me like he appears to be against you fellers. I'd advise the lot of you to stay away from the inquest and stay out of town till things cool down a bit. There's no sense in looking for trouble."

Preston considered, his eyes brooding. Abruptly a crafty gleam appeared in their dark depths.

"Hatfield," he said, "I've a notion what you said makes sense. Okay, you take over the chore, but keep away from Kimble. No sense in taking chances."

"I'll try not to take too many," Hatfield promised.

Hatfield left the ranch early the following morning. His eyes were grimly exultant as he rode for Cuevas.

"Goldy, I've got him placed at last," he told the sorrel. "He's older and thinner than when I saw him in Arizona, but that's to be expected. It's more than ten years since I saw him kill Tom White in Galeyville with that infernal double cross-pull of his. He put two slugs between White's eyes and the holes weren't an inch apart. Yes, that's who he is — Curly Bill Graham, the coldest killer Arizona ever knew, the leader of the Graham gang. The man Wyatt Earp thought he killed with a load of buckshot in the breast over at Iron Springs, west of Tombstone. Lots of folks always declared that Graham didn't die, that he recovered from his wounds and trailed his twine because Arizona was at last getting too hot to hold him and his bunch. Looks like they were right. Well, I've a notion we'll know before the day is out. This may not be just the proper way for a peace officer to handle the situation, but if I let him run around loose much longer he'll do for some other poor devil and likely as not that poor devil will be me. If we ever have a showdown with the time and place of his own choosing, I won't have a chance. The man doesn't live who can shade that draw of his, but after watching him in action that day in Galeyville I figured he's got a weakness, a little one, but a weakness just the same. He gets set, and shoots where he looks. That's the way I've got him figured out. If I've figured right, I have a chance and everything will be okay. If I'm wrong, everything will be okay, too. For I'll be dead and won't have to worry about it. June along, horse, we've got things to do."

Face bleak, eyes coldly gray, Jim Hatfield rode on to his rendezvous with death.

19

Upon reaching Cuevas, Hatfield immediately repaired to the sheriff's office.

"Here's the answer to your message to McDowell," Raines announced, handing Hatfield a sealed envelope.

Hatfield tore open the envelope and swiftly read the contents, his eyes glowing. Without comment, he passed it to Raines who spelled it out with muttering lips.

"Well, I'll be a lizard!" he exploded exultantly. "Looks like we've got a line on our man at last. So the dirty buzzard served time in Arizona for stealing cows. I always knew he was off-color."

"Yes," Hatfield agreed, "but it may not mean much. Because a man has made a slip, and paid for it, doesn't mean he's going to keep on raising hell. Many a reckless young feller has got himself in hot water, paid a hard price for it, and ended up an admired and respected citizen. I've known cases like that, and so have you. It may be the case with Brant Preston. The case report on him states that he was a model prisoner, was paroled and worked steadily for three years, after which he was able to buy a small mortgaged spread. He paid off the mortgage and when he left Arizona for Texas, he was well thought of in the community. He came here with a clean slate and so far as anybody knows for sure, he's kept it clean."

The sheriff growled and mumbled. "See the report says he has oiler blood on his mother's side," he commented.

"Spanish," Hatfield corrected. "His mother's father was a Spanish emigrant to Mexico. There's nothing wrong with Spanish blood of the right sort. Don't let your silly prejudice against Mexicans run away with your judgment."

The sheriff looked puzzled but did not appear impressed. "See there's nothing much on Cartina," he observed.

"Except his mother's name before she married his father," Hatfield replied with a touch of grimness. "Remember that name, Raines. It may mean something to you before the day is out. Something that may take your mind off Brant Preston."

The sheriff looked puzzled, but Hatfield did not see fit to elaborate at the moment.

"When's that inquest to be held?" he asked.

"In about half an hour," Raines replied. "Going to attend and see 'em turn that killer loose again?"

"Figure to," Hatfield replied briefly.

There being but one body to deal with, the inquest was held in Doc McChesney's office. It didn't last long. Half a dozen witnesses reluctantly testified that Kimble had to shoot if he wanted to stay alive. The verdict being a foregone conclusion, Hatfield left before it was rendered. He crossed to Flintlock Finnegan's saloon and stood leaning against the bar, facing the swinging doors.

Ten minutes passed and Pierce Kimble came through the doors. Hatfield stepped to the middle of the room and stood facing him. Kimble also halted, staring questioningly with his dead-looking eyes. His feet were wide apart, planted solidly, his spear-point hands hung limply at his sides. The room was abruptly deadly still. Hatfield's voice rang loud through the silence, like steel grinding on ice, bared with contempt —

"Hello, murderer!" he called. "Looking for another slow old man to kill?"

Pierce Kimble's long body stiffened. His black eyes crawled with reddish fires. The Ranger's voice bit at him again —

"Reckon Tombstone got to have a sort of final sound for you, didn't it? So you came east to find — a *grave, Bill Graham!*"

For a paralyzed instant men stood gasping at the voicing of the notorious outlaw's name. Then there was a wild scramble to get out of line.

Up and across flashed Kimble's hands in the double cross-pull no man had ever beaten or even equalled.

Jim Hatfield, lightning fast though he knew himself to be, did not try to beat it. His slender hands did not move, but his body did. He hurled himself sideways before he reached. Kimble's two bullets yelled through the space Hatfield had

158

occupied a split second before. Weaving, ducking, dodging, Hatfield went across the room directly at Kimble's flaming guns. His own Colts were roaring a hurricane blast of sound. Blood spurted from his cheek where one of Kimble's bullets had grazed the flesh. His hat was swept from his head. One shirt sleeve was ripped to shreds.

The lances of flame gushing from his gun muzzles seemed to center on Kimble's breast, the sledge-hammer blows of the striking slugs literally lifting the killer from his feet and blasting him into eternity with his fingers still twitching on the triggers of his empty guns. He crashed to the floor at Hatfield's feet, one spear-head hand reaching toward the Lone Wolf's boot.

The saloon was a pandemonium. Men were yelling, shouting, laughing hysterically.

"Did you ever see anything like it?"

"He walked right smack into them bullets and dodged 'em comin'!"

"Hell, he was just givin' Kimble a chance; he could have thrown his guns up in the air, caught 'em comin' down and plugged Pierce before he could clear leather!"

"Gents, that was shootin'!"

Hatfield and Sheriff Raines, who had just rushed in, knelt beside the dead man and turned him over on his back. Flintlock Finnegan stooped down to voice a question —

"Feller, was he really Bill Graham?"

Hatfield silently opened the dead man's shirt

and stared at the mass of puckered scars marking his breast.

"I don't know for sure," he admitted, "but he had eyes and hands and a grin like Graham and he drew crossways like Graham. You'll rec'lect Wyatt Earp always claimed he shot Graham in the breast with a double charge of buckshot. Well, those scars alongside his wishbone sure look to me like they were made by buckshot."

"They sure do," agreed the old saloon keeper. "What I'd like to know," he muttered to himself as he stood up, "big feller, who in the hell are *you!*"

Another inquest was held at once. This time witnesses clamored to be heard and eagerly swore that Kimble even fired the first shot.

"Okay, okay," said Doc McChesney as he directed a verdict of acquittal. "Getting to be a habit hereabouts, but I'll catch somebody some day, see if I don't."

Hatfield and the sheriff left together. "By gosh!" Raines suddenly exclaimed. "I get it — that name. *Graham!* That was the name of Fernando Cartina's mother before she married his Dad."

"Exactly," Hatfield replied.

"And so," began the sheriff.

"Yes, you should be able to figure that one out," Hatfield interrupted. "I wondered how long it would take you to tumble. But it may not mean a thing, just as Brant Preston once being in trouble may not mean a thing."

"Now I don't know what the Sam Hill to think!" wailed the sheriff.

"Don't try," Hatfield advised him wearily. "Things are getting worse mixed up all the time. I'm riding up to Cartina's place. Somebody should notify him of Kimble's death and I guess I'd better handle the chore."

"Want me to go with you, just in case?" asked Raines.

"Don't think it will be necessary," Hatfield declined the offer. "I'll see you later. By the way, how large a posse do you think you could get together in a hurry?"

"I reckon I can figure on about thirty gents of the right sort," the sheriff replied. "Why?"

"Because," Hatfield replied slowly, "I've a hunch I may need one in a hurry before long."

Hatfield had no trouble reaching Fernando Cartina's big white *casa*. He found the ranch and mine owner at home and received a cordial invitation to come in. With a word of thanks he entered the ranchhouse, sat down and rolled a cigarette in silence. Cartina regarded him, an expression of polite curiosity on his dark and handsome face. Finally Hatfield broke the silence.

"Pierce Kimble is dead," he announced without preamble.

Cartina started and his hands gripped the arms of his chair till the knuckles whitened.

"Dead!" he repeated. "Why — why — when — how —"

161

"Cartina," Hatfield interrupted quietly. "I'm sorry I had to kill your half-brother."

Cartina paled. He wet his suddenly dry lips with the tip of his tongue.

"So — so — you — know," he breathed hoarsely.

"Yes," Hatfield replied. "I know your mother's name was Graham and that Curly Bill Graham was her son by her first marriage."

Don Fernando sat staring straight in front of him, his face haggard, his eyes tortured. "We were boys together," he said dully at last. "My mother loved him. He was the elder, but I was always the steadier. Before she died, she begged me to try and look after him. He came here after Wyatt Earp nearly killed him. Most people believed Earp *did* kill him. I guess it would have been better if he had."

"Yes, very much better," Hatfield agreed. "I suppose you realize that you were harboring and protecting an outlaw and killer."

"I promised my mother," *Don* Fernando repeated in the same full, hopeless voice. Suddenly he raised his head defiantly.

"Bill wasn't a fugitive from justice," he declared. "There were no warrants out for him in Arizona."

"I guess you're right about that," Hatfield agreed soberly. "He and his bunch had connections over there and plenty of political pull. And he left before his friends fell from power."

"I really believe he stayed straight while he was

over here," Cartina said. "He was in trouble, yes. He couldn't seem to keep his hands away from his guns. But he was never held for a killing. Strange that he should die by a bullet, after all. I would have never believed the man lived who could kill him in a fair fight."

The shadow of a smile crossed Hatfield's sternly handsome face. "How do you know he was killed in a fair fight?" he asked.

Don Fernando looked surprised. "I believe you said you killed him?" he stated rather than asked. Hatfield nodded.

Don Fernando smiled in turn, a rather wan smile. "Well, then," he said. "I guess Bill was killed in fair fight."

Hatfield inclined his black head. "Thank you, suh," he said simply.

Cartina nodded acknowledgment. "Yes, I believe he stayed straight over here," he repeated. "He was my right-hand man with the mines and my ranch. He handled all my book work."

"Knew all the details of your business, then," Hatfield remarked.

"Of course. I relied on his advice. I'll miss him a lot." He shrugged and threw out his hands in an expressive Latin gesture.

"What's done is done," he said. "It is *kismet!*"

"Yes," Hatfield conceded gravely. "I guess Fate does take a hand in things, now and then. 'There is a Destiny that shapes our ends, rough hew them though we may.' "

Cartina regarded him curiously. "Hatfield,

163

you're a strange man — for a wandering cowhand," he remarked.

Hatfield smiled a little. "Yes, for a wandering cowhand."

Cartina sighed, and stood up. "You will stay for dinner, of course?" he invited. Hatfield nodded.

"Good," said the ranchowner. "Pardon me while I make arrangements." With a nod he left the room. Hatfield heard him walking to the back of the house.

The moment he had entered it, Hatfield took notice of the big and elaborately furnished room. Now he swiftly crossed to where a rifle lay on antler prongs above the fireplace. He took down the weapon, quickly examined the breech and replaced it, the concentration furrow deepening between his black brows.

Hatfield enjoyed a good dinner with Cartina, and shook hands when they parted. There was a baffled look in his green eyes as he rode away from the big ranchhouse.

"Why," he asked of nobody in particular, "why do two jiggers have to have brand-new firing pins in their rifles at the same time?"

20

It was late when Hatfield left Cartina's ranch-house. He decided to spend the night in town and found the place humming. The news of Tom Garrett's rescue from the Mexican jail had gotten around, Garrett having ridden into town with his daughter late that afternoon. Hatfield was the recipient of admiring glances and deluged with compliments by Garrett's many friends. Men who had formerly had nothing but hard things to say of Brant Preston were now singing his praises.

Hatfield found Lonnie Garrett at a table in Finnegan's place.

"Won't you sit down?" she invited cordially. "I'm waiting for Dad, we're heading back to the ranch in a little while. He wanted to come in and say hello to his friends. And I want to thank you for bringing him back to me."

"I just went along with the boys," Hatfield deprecated.

"Yes," she replied gravely, "and if you hadn't gone along, I think Dad would still be down there in that horrible jail. Again I want to thank you, for him and for me. If there's ever anything I can do —"

"There's something you can do right now," Hatfield interrupted. "You can make me a promise."

"Granted, even before you tell me what it is," was the instant reply.

"Okay," Hatfield said. "I want you to promise me not to marry Brant Preston till I give the word. I know, you told him you would if he brought your dad back, but there are always ways a woman can put things off for a bit. Is it a bargain?"

The girl's piquant face had abruptly gone tense, her eyes somber.

"I — I promise," she said, her voice hardly above a whisper. "I don't know why you ask, but I promise. I could hardly say no to you after what you did for me."

"Thanks," Hatfield said. "I don't want you marrying anybody just yet. Preston, nor — Fernando Cartina."

Lonnie's eyes widened. "Why — why," she faltered, "what makes you say *that?*"

Hatfield smiled, his even teeth flashing white, his green eyes sunny.

"I've got pretty good eyes," he said. "I think I can tell what a woman is thinking when she looks at a man."

Lonnie stared at him a moment. Abruptly she rose to her feet.

"Dad is at the door, calling me," she said. "I have to go." Her gaze met his squarely. The suspicion of a dimple showed at one corner of her red mouth.

"I wonder," she said softly, "just how good your eyes really are?"

She was gone before he could frame a reply. He gazed after her, a slightly bewildered look in the eyes she had mentioned.

"Now what the devil did she mean by that?" he demanded querulously.

"Hard to tell," said Flintlock Finnegan over his shoulder. "Hard to tell what a woman means or don't mean."

Hatfield flushed, realizing that he had spoken aloud.

They buried Bob Whetsall in the Cuevas graveyard alongside the man who killed him. Sheriff Raines promised to try and locate any kin the old fellow might have left.

Hatfield was curious as to just what his reception would be at the Circle P, having learned that Hilton had been in town during the day and had heard of the killing of Pierce Kimble.

Little Crowley was loud in his congratulations. Hilton and Kearns regarded him with grudging admiration and respect. Brant Preston's eyes were inscrutable, but his face wore a relieved expression.

"I'm glad that sidewinder is out of the picture," he said. Hatfield had a feeling he meant it.

Day after day, Hatfield rode the Circle P range. Also, unknown to the Circle P waddies and Preston, he rode through the many little river villages that hugged the banks of the Rio Grande. In the role of a wandering cowboy he drank in the *cantinas,* danced with dark-eyed *señoritas* and wagered on cock fights. Everywhere he was greeted with true Mexican courtesy and hospitality. The Lone Wolf had a way with him and the naive villagers confided many secrets, but the thing he sought eluded him. There was one subject the villagers would not discuss. Veiled allusions produced only tight-lipped silence. Over the apparently light-hearted little *pueblos* something ominous and terrible brooded. Hatfield could sense a tense expectancy, a waiting for something dreaded and feared to happen. It was like the lull that precedes the storm. Plainly the villagers were afraid. Afraid, and obsessed by portending events. Hatfield was worried and depressed.

Finally he gave up the villages and turned his attention to the Cingaro Trail. Through grim, bone-strewn Pardusco Canyon he followed the crooked track, losing himself amid the maze of branches that tortured through narrow gorges and side canyons, the thing he sought always eluding him. One night, as he sat Goldy in the shadow of a mesquite thicket, a large band of riders thundered past, the irons of their horses striking sparks from the stones. He tried to follow the band, but a heavy rain was falling, washing out what little spoor they made, and the roar of white water in the canyon drowned the sound of hoofs. Somewhere amid the tangle of trails he lost them.

In the meanwhile, he found opportunity to

hold secret rendezvous with Sheriff Raines.

"Have you noticed," said Raines, "that since you did for Pierce Kimble there hasn't been a hold-up or a robbery?"

Hatfield nodded. "Yes, I've thought about it," he admitted. "It sort of ties up with a theory I've developed apropos of that snake-eyed hellion and explains quite a few things that had me puzzled."

"Take that payroll for the Blansford mines up to the northeast," said the sheriff. "Went through disguised as a wagon-load of sugar and beans without a guard, and went through slick as a whistle. A month ago owlhoots would have rained out of the sky onto that wagon. Maybe Pierce was *El Hombre*," he hazarded hopefully.

Hatfield shook his head "Wish you were right," he replied, "but you're not. *El Hombre* is still very much alive and kicking as you're liable to realize any day."

"And you still can't figure out who he is?"

"I have a very good notion who *The Man* is," Hatfield replied. "But you can't take notions into court. They won't stand up when a good lawyer starts knocking the props from under them. I've still to get something definite on the hellion. That's what I'm trying to do. He's got a hangout somewhere this side of the River, I'm willing to swear to that. Until I find that hangout or we get an unexpected lucky break, he's got us hogtied. And I'm mightily afraid time's running short. A little while longer and all hell is liable to bust loose along the Border. I'm convinced of it after what Tom Garrett told me he heard while he was in jail. It's an open secret in Cheno's town that an uprising against Diaz is in the making and that money has been pouring down from this side of the Line. Well, all I can do is keep looking."

"Well, anyhow, things are a darn sight more peaceable right now than they've been hereabouts of late," said Raines.

"Uh-huh," nodded Hatfield, "but keep your eyes open. I've a prime notion they'll bust loose somewhere before long."

Hatfield was right.

During recent months, the Cuevas mine owners felt they had solved the problem of protecting their bullion shipments from the outlaws. After each monthly clean-up of the stamp mills, the metal — silver with a heavy gold content — was melted down and cast into 150-pound bricks, too heavy and unwieldy for packing off on horseback. The bricks were transported to Crater and the railroad in a ponderous freight wagon with a driver and a guard. A quarter of a mile behind, keeping their distance, rode four more guards, spaced out and armed with rifles and revolvers. If an attempt were made on the treasure wagon, the guards would quickly know it and would be able to overtake the heavily burdened horses of the robbers. The simple but ingenious plan had worked.

The driver and guard of the rumbling wagon were in a placid frame of mind a few days after

Hatfield and Raines had their pow-pow when the clumsy vehicle neared Pardusco Creek, a swift and fairly shallow stream that ran through Pardusco Canyon and finally emptied into the Rio Grande. A wooden bridge spanned the creek about fifteen miles east of Cuevas.

The horses' hoofs rang loudly on the boards as the wagon rolled onto the bridge. Suddenly there was a loud crack, then a grinding and splintering followed by wild yells of alarm from guard and driver, and finally a rending crash and a prodigious splash.

Drenched and sputtering, the guard and the driver slid off the tilted seat and into the water. Raving curses, they sloshed through the shallow water to try and get the fallen horses onto their feet before they drowned.

From the thick chaparral growth that flanked the bridge on either side burst a storm of gunfire. Guard and driver went down, kicking and thrashing. The driver managed to stagger erect and attempt to claw his way up the steep bank. Another volley brought him down again to lie half in and half out of the water.

Down the bank leaped four men. Heaving and tugging, they got the heavy ingots from the partially submerged wagon. The harness-entangled horses were callously left to drown.

The guards riding a quarter of a mile behind the wagon heard the shooting. They put spurs to their horses and raced for the creek. No living thing was in sight when they reached the scene of robbery and murder, but the surface of a faint trail flowing south-westward through a narrow opening in the growth was scarred with hoof marks.

"After the hellions!" yelled one. "That's the way they went. They can't get in the clear packin' six hundred pounds of metal."

"Wait!" roared the leader of the guards, a crafty old frontiersman. "That may be a blind lead. Nick, you slide across the crik and see if there are any hoof marks over there. This looks funny to me. No, no use tryin' to do anything for poor Hank and George. They're shot to pieces. Snake-blooded skunks! Hustle, Nick."

Nick sent his horse foaming through the shallow water and clambering up the opposite bank. Back and forth he ranged, leaning low in his saddle, peering and probing.

"Nary a sign of a horse over here," he shouted.

"Come on!" yelled the leader. "After the side-winders!"

The troop raced south, following the trail of the hoof marks.

"Watch them prints close," cautioned the leader." Watch for signs of the skunks stopping to hide the bricks in the brush.

They covered a mile with the prints still showing plainly in the soft surface of the trail, but with no sign of the quarry. The mile became two, then increased to three. The bronks were beginning to blow. But still the marks left by half a dozen swiftly moving horses flowed on ahead.

The old leader jerked his foaming mount to a halt. The others followed suit, chattering questions.

"Blazes! Can't you see we've been flim-flammed?" the oldster exploded. "Those bronks ahead ain't packing anything but two-legged snakes. They'd never been able to keep ahead of us for this far if they were packing the metal, too."

"Maybe they loaded the metal onto led horses," hazarded a fresh-faced young fellow.

"You infernal jackass!" snorted the old leader. "Don't you know a bunch stickin' together can't go no faster than the slowest horse? A horse loaded with one of them gold bricks would be off his stride all the time holding up the rest of the bunch. And all those prints are clean-cut and even. A horse that's loaded and led shambles. A horse with his head up doesn't. We'll never catch 'em and they know it. Back to the bridge and see if by any chance they hid the stuff in the brush there. If they did, they'll have snuk it out and gone with it, but we might still be able to catch 'em up."

However, a thorough search of the vicinity of the bridge convinced the old-timer that nothing had been secreted there, and it was plain that no horses had come and gone while they were following the trail south.

"Shall we haul those poor devils out of the water?" asked one of the guards.

"Leave 'em where they are," the oldster replied glumly. "It won't hurt 'em to get a little wetter. And I want the sheriff to see things just like they are. This business is going to look mighty funny to anybody that wasn't hereabouts when it happened. We don't want some suspicious galoot to get to wondering if maybe us fellers might have sort of taken our time getting here. I've heard of such things. Let's go!"

Jim Hatfield was in Cuevas when the four guards arrived on their near-exhausted horses. Sheriff Raines immediately swore in a posse.

"You come along, too, Hatfield," he directed. "You might get a chance to put that shootin' ability of yours to some use."

The shadows were lengthening when they reached the fallen bridge, but otherwise things were just as the four guards had left them. The posse dismounted and nosed about.

"Stringers sawed nearly through," grunted the sheriff, pointing to the end of one of the horizontal timbers that had supported the span. The upper section was clean-cut, the lower quarter splintered.

Hatfield nodded. "Left just enough wood uncut to hold the weight of the span," he remarked. "The added weight of the wagon sent it down."

"But where in Sam Hill did they go with the bricks?" somebody wanted to know.

Hatfield did not answer. He was staring at the hurrying water that sloshed and swirled about the lifeless bodies of men and horses. His gaze drifted upstream, his black brows knitted.

"Come along for a look-see," he told the sheriff. "Tell the rest of the bunch to stay back so they won't be tramping out any signs that may have been left."

The sheriff relayed the order. Hatfield led the way to the very lip of the bank, threading his way slowly through the brush, his eyes never leaving the soft earth where the low bank shelved down. They covered a dozen yards or so and the Ranger suddenly halted with an exclamation.

"Look" he told the sheriff, pointing to a wedge-shaped indenture in the earth just above the water's edge.

"What is it?" asked the sheriff, peering through the shadows.

Hatfield did not answer. His eyes were following a line from the narrow inner tip of the opening up the bank.

"And look there," he said, pointing to a stout tree that grew a few feet back from the crest of the bank. "Look at the trunk, Jed. What do you see?"

The sheriff peered close. "Bark's scuffed off," he said. "Looks to me like a horse was tied to that tree by a lead rope and did considerable jerking and straining. Uh-huh, there was a rope tied to that trunk, and plumb recent. I'd swear to it."

"Right," Hatfield replied grimly. "But there wasn't a horse tied to the other end of the rope."

"What the devil was then?" demanded the puzzled sheriff.

"Oh, just a boat," the Ranger replied with elaborate casualness.

"A boat!"

"Uh-huh, the boat the hellions had cached here. The boat they used to float the metal downstream."

The sheriff swore like a madman as the light dawned.

"Those guards figured six men did the chore," Hatfield went on. "Four were holed up in the brush. The other two were up here ready to cast off. By the time the wagon was in the creek and the guard and driver done for, they would have had the boat floated down and ready for the stuff to be loaded into it. Then they sailed merrily down the creek, leaving the other four to lay a cold trail on that track that veers away from the stream for the guards to follow. Sort of cute, eh? Still think *El Hombre* died when Pierce Kimble turned up his toes?"

The sheriff swore some more and voiced a reply that was becoming habitual with him of late, "I don't know what the hell to think!"

"One thing's sure for certain," Hatfield said. "All the brains didn't pass on with Kimble. This was about as smart a trick as I ever heard tell of. Well, come along, we might as well head back for town. No following a trail in the water, and there are a hundred places where they could unload, even if they didn't keep right on going till they reached the Rio Grande, which is just as likely. Let's go."

The dejected posse rode home through the growing darkness. Sheriff Raines fumed and cursed under his moustache, but Jim Hatfield was grimly silent.

And in a snug hideout along the Pardusco Trail, a bloated spider of a man with beady black eyes and a merciless mouth stroked the ponderous metal bricks with greedy hands and chuckled softly to himself.

"*Maldito!* this is the great help," he said to a companion who sat across the table from him, sombrero pulled low over his eyes, *serape* muffled about his chin. "*Si,* it is enough! Soon, very soon, we will be ready to strike. Your men they are ready? *Bueno!* Ha! I, Juan Cheno, Ruler of Mexico! I will be the great man, *amigo mio,* and you will be, after me, the greatest man in the land."

Intent on the precious metal, he did not see the derisive smile that twisted the other's thin lips nor the mockingly amused glint in his eyes.

21

Hatfield continued to ride the Cingaro Trail, prowling the side canyons, striking into the hills at times — searching, searching! He came upon quite a few lonely, deserted cabins where prospectors had burrowed industriously into the hillsides or the banks of little streams. Sometimes there was evidence that the gold seekers had acquired modest wealth. More often the story was one of disappointment or tragedy with rusting tools amid the ruins of a caved-in shaft or tunnel. Once or twice he found moldering bones.

One day he approached a little clearing at no great distance from the main trail. Suddenly he heard a sound unusual to the lonely fastnesses — the sound of a human voice. He paused to listen.

Again it came, faint, hollow. It *was* a voice, fraught with terror and despair. Over and over a single Spanish word croaked —

"*Avyuda! Avyuda!* Help! Help!"

Hatfield rode forward swiftly, shouting as he rode. He tried to locate the sound but it was elusive, apparently coming from the ground beneath his horse's hoofs. Abruptly he pulled Goldy to a halt once more and swung from the saddle. He had caught sight of the earth-ringed, yawning mouth of an ancient mine shaft.

"Looks like some poor devil's fallen down that

hole," he muttered, hastening toward the opening. "Hold on, pardner," he shouted, "I'm coming pronto!"

He reached the shaft and peered down it. For a tense moment he hung over the dank hole, his flesh crawling, a sick burn at the pit of his stomach. Unconsciously he drew back, a slight shiver twitching his broad shoulders.

"God! is there anything they *won't* do?" he breathed. He leaned over the shaft lip again, his face grim.

"Don't move, feller," he called in Spanish. "Take it easy where you are. I'll get you out some way! For God's sake, *don't move!*"

The shaft was scarcely more than eight feet deep with a smooth, damp floor. It was some six feet in diameter. At the bottom a man pressed his scrawny body against the crumbling dirt wall. He stood utterly motionless on bare feet, his ragged pantaloons rolled above his knees, his arms bound tightly to his sides by turn on turn of rawhide. He was evidently on the verge of collapse from exhaustion and fear. He stood utterly motionless in his strained position.

On the floor of the shaft, restlessly moving, gliding here and gliding there, vainly seeking escape from their prison were fully a dozen huge mountain rattlesnakes. From time to time one slithered over the miserable captive's bare foot or brushed against the shrinking flesh of his leg.

"Don't move," Jim cautioned again, knowing that so long as he stood like a statue he was fairly safe from the reptiles. But let him shift a foot or reel from exhaustion and the needle-sharp fangs, dripping venom like brown ink, would be plunged into his flesh.

For a moment, the Ranger stood racking his brain. He half drew one of his guns, then let it fall back in its holster. He might shoot all of the snakes despite the difficult angle and the uncertain light, but the risk of wounding them instead of killing them outright was too great. The rattlers, lashing about in pain and terror, were almost certain to strike the hapless *peon*. No, he couldn't take such chances. There was but one thing to do.

Searching about, he found a stout club. He hefted it for weight, ran his eye along it in quest of a flaw in the wood and found none. Next he called Goldy, unlooped his riata and made sure that it was tied hard and fast. For an instant he was tempted to try and drop the loop over the *peon's* shoulders and jerk him out of the pit before the snakes could strike, but again he decided the risk was too great. Had the man's arms not been bound it would have been comparatively simple, but as it was, there was always the chance that the noose might slip and the helpless victim fall back on top of the snakes. No, there was but one thing to do.

"Steady, horse," he cautioned. Wrapping the rope about one arm and holding the club, he raised his hands high above his head and leaped into that pit of horror.

He landed squarely on a big rattler, smashing the life out of it instantly. Another threw itself into a loose fold and struck with lightning speed. The fangs clashed harmlessly against the tough leather of the Ranger's boot. The club swept down and beat the snake to death before it could strike again.

Back against the helpless *peon,* shielding him from a chance stroke, the Lone Wolf fought a nightmare battle in that pit of hell. All about him buzzed and hissed the aroused reptiles. Time and again they struck, and time and again his boots or his chaps saved him. He was pretty sure that none of the rattlers could strike above the protecting leather, but he was not certain and the possibility made his flesh crawl. One huge fellow, rearing high, lashed at the club as it descended. His long fangs stabbed the tough wood a scant inch from the Ranger's hand — so close in fact that the released venom splashed over his fingers.

Hatfield soon was dripping with sweat and he thought he would suffocate in the close air of the pit, reeking as it was with the horrible stench of the reptiles. Again and again he struck, his arm aching and burning with fatigue, his nerves taut to the breaking point. It seemed to him that the devilish things multiplied with each blow. In a red haze he slashed and pounded and stamped in that nightmare inferno of writhing bodies and gaping jaws.

Abruptly he realized that he was pounding a dead snake to a pulp. There were no more live reptiles left to face him. Gasping for breath, he turned to the captive. The *peon* suddenly gave a choking cry and grovelled against the wall. Hatfield followed his bulging eyes and saw a last rattler, dying with a broken back, lying across the man's foot. He saw also the ominous twin punctures where the fangs had pierced the naked ankle in a last convulsive movement. Cursing bitterly, he ground the snake's head to fragments with his boot heel. Then he draped the *peon's* sagging body across his shoulder and went up the rope hand over hand, Goldy snorting and bearing back against the lunging weight.

Reaching the ground, Hatfield slashed the rawhide thongs that bound the *peon's* arms, laid him on the ground and went to work on the wound. He applied a tourniquet made with a handkerchief, slashed the fang punctures crisscross, laid his lips to the wound and sucked out as much blood as possible. A little stream ran through the clearing and in this he dipped his neckerchief and applied it to the wound as a wet dressing to stimulate draining.

The *peon* was nearly unconscious from the pain, terror and exhaustion. He was a scrawny little fellow with soft brown eyes and the mouth of an abused child. Hatfield stared down at him compassionately. He knew the kind — there were many, many like him in the river villages — children, despite their years of manhood, who needed care and gentle supervision, in them the making of good citizens. Looking after such people and seeing to it that they received justice was part of a Ranger's work. Easily influenced, they were a potential asset or liability to the state according to whose hand shaped them.

"And of late there's been too many devil-claws tending to the job!" the Ranger growled, his face bleak.

Almost hidden in a tangle of burr oaks was a deserted mine cabin, old, dilapidated, but still secure against wind and weather. Hatfield found it to be furnished with a rusty little stove, a rickety table, chairs and a bunk built against the wall. He cut boughs, filled the bunk with them and spread his saddle blanket over them, making a fairly comfortable bed for the patient. He got a fire going in the stove and heated water in a battered tin bucket he unearthed. He had a little food in his saddlebags and a small skillet.

There was a chance, he knew, that the fiends who had placed the *peon* in the snake pit might come back to see how their victim was faring, but he decided to risk it. He rather relished the idea of a brush with them, in fact, and his lean jaw set tight as his slim bronzed hands caressed the butts of his heavy Colts. He loosely tethered Goldy deep in the pine grove where he could graze and roll and still be safe from observation. Then he went back to spend the night tending to the wants of his patient. Wise in the ways of the forest, he brewed a draft from the roots, leaves and berries he gathered and forced the injured man to swallow it.

The drink had an almost immediate effect. A little color crept back into the sallow face; the lips lost their ghastly gray tinge. The man opened his eyes and stared at Hatfield uncomprehendingly at first. Then remembrance flooded his brain and he struggled to sit up.

"Take it easy, old-timer," Hatfield soothed him. "You're all right now — nothing to worry about. Just take it easy."

Still the *peon* struggled to speak. Finally the words came, sliding over his stiff lips in a froth of terror.

"Rosa!" he gasped, "*Mujer* — Rosa!"

Jim leaned closer. "What about your wife Rosa?" he asked.

The black eyes were like those of a hunted animal. "*El Caballeros!* They ride to Canales! They take her — kill!"

For a moment the Ranger sat silent, thinking furiously. Canales was a river village, many hours of hard riding distant. It would take him all night to reach the little *pueblo* and rescue the woman from the vengeance of the Riders. He very much feared that if left alone during the night the *peon* would die. There was also the deadly danger that the devils who placed him in the snake pit might return, seek him out and finish him. His life was too valuable to risk, for Hatfield was confident that in the man he had the key to *El Hombre* and *El Hombre*'s hidden stronghold. No, there was too much at stake, he could not leave the *peon* for the night — there had to be another way.

184

Suddenly he exclaimed sharply under his breath. "Why didn't I think of it before!" he exulted. "Tom Garrett'll be glad to hustle down to Canales and do this little chore for me. He can grab off the girl and take her back to the Bowtie with him. She'll be safe there — nobody'll know about her. Yes, that's the ticket.

"Your name, *amigo?*" he questioned, "and just where does your wife live in Canales?"

"The house on the little hill by the river — the first house when one rides from the east," whispered the other. "You will save her, *Señor?* Me, I am Doreto."

"Yeah, I'll see she's taken care of," Hatfield promised simply. "Now you just take another swallow of this stuff and go to sleep. I'll be back in a little while — just take it easy."

The Bowtie ranchhouse was less than an hour's fast riding from the canyon. Hatfield made Goldy sift sand and there was still a glow of the sunset above the western peaks when he pulled up at the Bowtie, swung to the ground and hurried up the veranda. Light steps sounded in answer to his knock and Lonnie Garrett opened the door. She gave a little cry of pleasure at sight of her visitor.

"Your dad in?" Hatfield asked, after greeting her. "I want to see him, right away."

"He is in Cuevas," Lonnie replied. "He and the boys rode in this afternoon. They won't be back until late; I'm all by myself except for Teresa, the cook."

185

22

For a tense moment Hatfield stared at Lonnie
Garrett, his whole plan tumbling about his ears.
The girl sensed something was wrong and her
face grew anxious.

"Wh-what is it?" she asked. "You're worried
about something."

Hatfield hesitated an instant before speaking.
Then he decided to take a chance. In terse sen-
tences he told her what had happened and held
out his Ranger badge.

Lonnie did not appear particularly surprised.
"So that's it," she said. "For some time I've
thought you were considerably more than you
pretended to be. I wonder that others haven't
thought so, too."

"Perhaps they have," Hatfield replied a trifle
grimly. "So you can understand how important
it is for me to get back and stay with that poor
devil tonight. But I can't let him down where his
wife is concerned. I promised him I'd look out
for her. Do you think you could make it to
Cuevas in time to round up your father and send
him to Canales?"

"No," Lonnie instantly replied, "You know
very well it couldn't be done. I'm not even going
to try. You wait here."

"What the devil you going to do?" Hatfield

called as she darted out the door and down the veranda steps.

"I'm going to Canales," she flung back at him. "Wait till I get a saddle on my horse."

She was at the corral whistling a clear note before he caught up with her.

"You can't do that, Lonnie," he protested as a clean-limbed little pinto came trotting to the bars, whinnying a question. "You can't take such a chance. You're just as liable as not to run into those damned Riders."

"I'm taking it," she replied briefly, flinging down the corral bars. "If you can take the chances you do for people who are practically unknown to you, I can take one for — for those who mean a great deal to me."

Her cheeks were bright with color as she finished, but she smiled up at him, led the pony to the stable and flung the hull onto his back.

"Your deal," the Ranger applauded briefly. "All right, little lady, have it your own way. But you'll have to take a spare horse along for the girl to ride — can't take any chances on your pony carrying double, you might have to make a run for it. No, wait, I've got a better notion. Will your pony follow with you on another horse?"

"Yes," she replied, "He's trained to."

"All right, that's fine." He whistled to Goldy. "He'll take you there faster than anything in Texas. Don't run your own horse to death; hold Goldy in and give him a chance. You've got time to make it, I'm sure. Those other hellions won't hustle — they'll figure they've got all the time in the world."

"Get my rifle from over the mantel and put it in the boot in place of yours," said Lonnie. "Mine is lighter and I handle it better. There are spare saddles in the barn, that roan over there is a good pony — take him."

Hatfield held the stirrup and she flung herself into the saddle. Her skirt rumpled upward showing her slim, beautiful legs and a white flash of her shapely thighs.

"Extremely revealing," she said, with a giggle, tugging futilely at the unruly skirt, "but I'm darned if I'll take time to change."

"A little more of this and I'll forget all about everything else and ride with you," Hatfield declared.

Lonnie flashed him a glance through her lashes. "Well —" she said. "No, I guess you'd better not. We have others to think about, and you are — distracting! Be seeing you, Jim."

She bent over swiftly and kissed him squarely on the mouth. Then she was gone with a clash of racing hoofs, her red curls tossing in the wind.

Hatfield gazed after her and sighed. "A certain jigger is darn lucky," he remarked with conviction, "and, darn it! I'm sorry it isn't me!"

He watched her out of sight, then he roped the roan, saddled up and headed back to the canyon cabin and his all night vigil with the patient.

The girl raced through the lovely blue dusk, the shimmer of the stars and then the silvery flood of the moonlight keeping her company as the miles unrolled their white ribbon behind her. Midnight came and went. The great clock in the sky wheeled on from east to west. Clouds began veiling the moon at times and the prairie grew shadowy and mysterious. Finally the pale gleam of the river showed on her left. Another half hour and she slowed the sorrel. Directly ahead was the village of Canales. On a little knoll loomed the hut of Doreto, the *peon*. It was silent and dark. Lonnie wondered if she were in time or if the raiders had already done their work. The cold stillness of death seemed to brood over the little home.

But when she knocked on the barred door, a frightened voice answered. Quickly she explained to the Mexican girl. A moment later Doreto's wife slipped through the doorway.

She was a shy little thing with great dark eyes that were now black pools of terror, but with Indian stoicism she accepted the danger that threatened her.

"*Si*, I can ride," she answered Lonnie's question. "I am ready."

She mounted lithely and took the reins Lonnie handed her.

"Hush!" she exclaimed. "Some one comes!"

Lonnie heard it too — the pound of swift hoofs ascending the knoll. Out of the shadows loomed ghostly riders, barring the way.

"Halt!" a voice shouted in Spanish.

Instantly the red-haired girl went into action.

"Follow me!" she screamed to the *peon* woman. Dropping the reins on Goldy's neck, knowing that the intelligent horse would know what to do, she jerked her rifle from the boot and charged straight at the approaching group, the saddle gun streaming flame.

There was a yell of pain and fear, a confused trampling of hoofs as the horses shied away from the spurts of fire and the screeching bullets. Another man shrieked in agony and pitched from the saddle. His horse wheeled and fled madly, adding to the confusion. Before the astounded killers could catch their breath, the two girls were through their disordered ranks and scudding down the rise. Bullets and a volley of curses whined after them, but to Goldy's iron endurance the long hours of travel had meant nothing, while the pinto, which had carried no load, was comparatively fresh. Behind them the click of hoofs soon died to a whisper of sound and ceased altogether. With the red dawn flaming behind them and the blue ripple of the wind tossed grasses in front, the two girls rode to the distant Bowtie and safety.

"I'll just wager he will be proud of me now!" Lonnie whispered to herself. Her cheeks were bright with color and her eyes dream-filled.

At the cabin in the canyon, Hatfield spent a busy night with his patient. Morning found the *peon* weak, in considerable pain, his leg much swollen, but alive. Not only had the Ranger's prompt and skillful doctoring saved his life, but he would not lose his leg. Leaving him sleeping fitfully, Jim scouted about the clearing and the grove and managed to knock over a brace of blue grouse with his six. He scoured the bucket thoroughly and made a broth which he fed to the patient. Then he risked a quick ride to the Bowtie ranchhouse. Tom Garrett was there. Garrett was well nigh bursting with pride at his daughter's exploit.

He shook hands warmly with Hatfield. "So you're a Ranger," he chuckled. "I might have known it. You do things like a Ranger. Don't hesitate to call on me for anything I can do. Gosh! I feel a sight better about things in this section. Guess we're due for a real clean-up."

"It isn't cleaned up yet," Hatfield told him.

"Nope, but it will be, it will be," Garrett declared with confidence. "I got to go down to the bunkhouse a minute. We'll eat when I come back." He stomped out, leaving Hatfield alone with the red-haired girl.

"I had to tell Dad," she said. "I figured some explanation was due him. I hope you don't mind."

"Of course not," Hatfield reassured her. "He can keep his mouth shut. And you're a real partner. You did yourself proud."

"Thank you, sir," Lonnie replied demurely. Hatfield had an uneasy feeling that she was laughing at him. He decided she needed taking down a peg.

"By the way," he said carelessly, "I believe

there's something I should give back to you."

"What?" Lonnie asked, falling into the trap.

"A kiss. Guess I owe you one."

Again the dark lashes fluttered down. "I've always heard an honest man pays his debts," she said softly.

Hatfield caught her up in his arms, lifting her clear off the floor. Her supple body pressed close to his, breast to breast. For a long moment their lips clung.

Old Tom Garrett came clattering up the veranda steps just then. If he noticed his daughter's heightened color he did not see fit to comment on it, but there was a twinkle in the back of his eyes and he certainly did not appear displeased.

After eating, Hatfield rode back to the canyon. "I'll bring him here as soon as he's strong enough to travel, if you don't mind," he told Garrett. "His wife can look after him and I figure he'll be safe here."

"You're darn right he will," Garrett promised emphatically. "I've got a Sharpe's buffalo gun ready for business and a couple of sixes."

Hatfield nodded. "So long, Lonnie, I'll be seeing you!" he said.

"A hard man to watch ride away," Garrett commented, with a sympathetic glance at his daughter.

"But a mighty easy one to watch ride back," she replied, leaving Garrett with something to think about.

The day and the night passed uneventfully in

the canyon. On the morning of the second day, Hatfield decided that the *peon* was strong enough to talk. Sitting beside him he questioned him gently. At first, terror filmed the dark eyes and the man would not answer. Gradually, however, under the hypnotic influence of the Lone Wolf's steady eyes and quiet voice, halting words came forth, became coherent, and steadied to a story fantastic, weird and amazing, a grim story of horror and cruelty, of towering, ruthless ambition and ingenious planning. No longer was the mystery of The Riders and *El Hombre* a mystery. The whole sinister business was now an open book to the lean, stern faced Lieutenant of Rangers. Now he had the information he needed. Already he was busy making a plan, a plan which would free the bloody triangle country from the dark blight that was settling over it and tear loose the cruel grip of the ill-omened nightflitting Riders and *El Hombre*.

23

Hatfield took the *peon* to the Bowtie. "You'll be safe here, and your wife, also," he assured him. "So you just wanted to leave the outfit for a while to look after your sick wife? And because of that they shoved you into that hole with the snakes and told you they were going to kill her. Well, quite a few snakes died in that hole the other day and I've a notion quite a few more are going to be handed a similar dose before long. Now let's once more go over the directions about how to get to their hangout."

Hatfield headed back to the Cingaro Trail. He paused first at the Bowtie storehouse for some things he felt he needed. Garrett had a good supply of dynamite on hand to be used for blowing waterholes. Hatfield stuffed his saddlebags with carefully wrapped sticks. He also took caps and a big coil of fuse.

Through grim Pardusco Canyon he rode, carefully checking certain landmarks. Finally he turned into a narrow, sunless gorge and continued warily. Just as the sunset was flaring golden behind the western peaks, he passed from the narrow neck into a wide, almost circular bowl ringed about by low cliffs, the hills soaring up beyond. The bowl was silent and deserted now, but the grass had been ground from the dusty earth by the endless passing and repassing of countless bare feet and the hoofs of many horses. Hatfield could imagine the brown ranks forming and reforming, going through endless military evolutions under grim, watchful eyes whose owners thought nothing of condemning a hapless bungler to the torture-death of cactus crucifixion or ant hill. He crossed the open space to the low cliffs on the far side. Here, after a little poking about, he found what he sought.

Partially concealed by bushes and vines was the dark opening of a cave. The sides and roof had been timbered. The floor was smooth and dry. Hatfield entered it, lighting a candle he had brought with him. A dozen steps farther on he paused and stared at what the flickering flame revealed.

Rifles, hundreds of them, new, carefully greased and stacked, and case after case of ammunition. From floor to timbered roof, the long rows stretched across the wide cave.

For minutes the Ranger gazed at the arms, visualizing what they meant. He saw the Border seething with blood and flame — murder, lust and robbery rampant, killings, torturing. He saw, too, what would come later — the thundering horses of the cavalrymen of the Union surging through the river villages, their sabres flashing in the sun, their pistols flaming in the night. The peaceful little river villages, no longer peaceful but lashed to a mad fury by cruelty and terror and the ruthless ambition of a twisted mind. Grimly the tall Ranger set about to thwart that ambition and prevent the horror that was in the making.

Carefully, skillfully, he planted his dynamite, concealing it from possible prying eyes and just as skillfully concealing the snaky length of fuse that ran from the cave to the summit of the low, slanting cliff. He calculated just how long it would take the fuse to burn and just how long it would take him to reach the narrow entrance of the clearing from the cliff top. The coil proved ample for the purpose.

Then, with the stage set for the drama that would be enacted the following night, he rode back to Cuevas.

There was excitement at Cuevas when he got there after midnight.

"They got the bank again!" a bartender told him excitedly. "Cleaned it out proper. Old Ab Carlysle wasn't there with his scattergun this time, poor ol' devil. Darnel did what he could but he was too slow. They bent a gun barrel over his head, tied up the clerks and took fifty thousand dollars. Jed Raines is chasin' them through the hills, but they got a good start and I won't calculate Jed has much chance."

Hatfield frowned at what he saw was liable to threaten the success of his plan. He was much relieved when Hipless Harley rode in a little later. Hipless had been to Crater and did not know about the robbery.

"Now listen close," Hatfield told him, "here's what I want you to do —"

He drew a map on the table top and explained in detail the route to the cliff-walled amphitheatre in the hills.

"It's up to you to find Raines and the posse and lead them there," he concluded. "Maybe you can run him down. I'll stay in Cuevas till the last minute on the chance of him coming back."

"And if he don't show up, you're ridin' into that nest of sidewinders by yourself?" Hipless asked in an awed voice.

"Yeah," the Lone Wolf replied simply. "It's my job, I'm figuring to hold me a one-man surprise party. So don't be too late!"

24

Hatfield visited Darnel, the bank cashier and acting president, who was at his desk. Darnel had a split scalp and a nasty headache but was otherwise in pretty good shape.

"This robbery is just about going to knock the props from under the bank, Hatfield," the cashier worried.

"Never mind," Jim reassured him. "I know where the money went. You'll have it all back inside of twenty-four hours. Maybe I'm in time to catch that bullion, too."

As long as he dared, Hatfield remained in Cuevas waiting for Sheriff Raines. Finally, as the afternoon shadows were growing long, he gave it up and rode swiftly north.

Dusk was falling when he reached the mouth of the gorge that led to the hidden amphitheatre. He did not use the canyon trail but sent Goldy straight through the hills. There he hid the sorrel in a thicket and made the last few hundred yards of the trip on foot. Crouched on the cliff top above the cave, he gazed at the strange scene in the bowl below, clearly outlined by many torches in the light of the full moon.

It was no longer empty. Marshalled in the trodden dust were fully five hundred *peons*. Silently they stood in lines of military precision, awaiting someone. They bore no arms, not even knives in their belts.

"Not takin' any chances with them till they're sure they've got them under their thumb," he muttered, his gaze centering on a tight group of men who stood near a number of horses that showed signs of hard riding. These men, dark of face, sinister of feature, he instantly knew were the dread Riders — messengers who were sent forth to summon the *peons* and who wreaked horrible vengeance upon any who refused their call. They were fully armed with rifle, revolver and knife.

"Those are the *hombres* I've got to look out for," Hatfield told himself. "The other poor devils down there'll be only too glad to bust loose. All they want to do is tend to their own business and live in peace."

He lifted his head at the click of hoofs drifting up from below. A moment later two men rode into the enclosure. One was short and squat with a bloated body and stringy black hair. He looked like a giant spider. The other, tall and straight, was muffled to his eyes in a dark *serape*. Hands snapped to salute at their entrance. The group of Riders, after saluting, turned and moved leisurely toward the mouth of the hidden cave.

"Going to get the guns and hand them out," Hatfield deduced. His face was grim and a trifle haggard as with steady hands cupped to shield the tiny flame, he touched a lighted match to the end of the coiled fuse. It sputtered, caught, and threw out a little shower of sparks which instantly vanished as the fire crept under the brush and leaves in which the coil was hidden. The length that dangled down the slanting cliff was also hidden by cunningly twisted vines. It was buried deep where it entered the cave.

"I haven't any choice in the matter," muttered the Ranger in self-justification. "Ten of those Riders are too much for me to try to handle by myself. One slip and everything would go to hell. If Raines and the posse were here it would be different."

As soon as the fuse was burning, he sped swiftly across the cliff tops and scrambled to the floor of the canyon. Loosening his guns in their holsters, he strode through the narrow gut and into the dusty bowl. On his broad breast gleamed the Star of the Rangers. His voice rolled in thunder between the rocky walls —

"Don't anybody make a move or it'll be his last! I have fifty men with rifles posted on top of the cliffs!"

The terrified *peons* broke ranks and huddled together, pointing, chattering, staring at the grim figure that stood, straight and tall, a dozen yards from the bloated spiderman and his blanket-swathed companion. Hatfield's voice rang out again —

"In the name of the State of Texas! I arrest Juan Cheno and Brant Preston, known as *El Hombre*, for robbery, murder, and inciting revolution on American soil. Anything you say may be used against you!"

The blanket dropped away revealing Brant Preston's darkly handsome face, now livid and contorted with rage and fear. Cheno let out a despairing squall —

"Miguel! Pedro! Felipe! To me — *pronto!*"

From the cave came an answering shout, a shout drowned by a crashing roar that shook the very mountains. A flare of reddish light dyed the hill ringed bowl the color of blood, followed by a rumbling of falling rocks, a splintering of timbers and a screech of terror that was cut off short. The cave mouth glowed with leaping flames that jerked and quivered to deafening volleys of shots. The heat of the burning timbers was setting off the thousands of cartridges stored in the cave.

The *peons*, remembering the Ranger's threat of rifles ringing the cliff tops, huddled together in a screaming mob, but Cheno and Preston realized what had actually happened and knew that the threat of rifles was a bluff. They went for their guns.

Weaving, ducking, firing with both hands, the Lone Wolf answered them shot for shot. Cheno crumpled up and lay still. Hatfield dashed away the blood that streamed into his eyes and lined sights on Preston's breast. His Colt bucked in his hand, again and again. He reeled as a slug tore through the flesh of his upper arm, steadied himself and fired his last cartridge. Preston's black muzzle yawned hungrily toward him.

But Preston did not fire. Over his face spread a look of vast surprise. The gun he held wavered, dropped from his nerveless hand. His knees bent under him as if he intended to kneel. Then he pitched forward on his face beside the dead Cheno. He did not move again.

Hatfield's head was whirling. Blood still seeped from a crease above his left temple and flowed freely from his gashed left arm. By an iron effort of the will, he got control of his reeling senses. Mechanically he reloaded his empty guns. His brain began clearing and when he turned to face the cowering *peons*, he was again steady on his feet. He holstered his guns and walked toward them with empty hands. In his strangely colored eyes was only kindness.

"Return to your homes, *amigos*," he said quietly. "You have nothing more to fear. I understand why you are here. *El Hombre* and his Riders are dead. Go home to your families, till the soil and live in peace."

They crowded around him, laughing, crying, clutching at his hands. Some of the more efficient hastened to bind up his wounds with the skill of much practice.

He was sitting with his back to a rock, alone, smoking a corn husk cigarette and feeling much better when Sheriff Raines and his dust-stained posse thundered through the gorge on near-exhausted horses.

"Are you all right, Jim?" the sheriff asked anxiously, leaping from his saddle and squatting beside the bandaged Ranger. "We got here as quickly as we could."

"Fine as frog hair," Hatfield assured him, adding whimsically. "But I'd sure take it kind if you'd get a fire going. There's some coffee and a bucket in my saddlebags. Right now I sure could stand a cup."

"Get busy with that coffee, some of you work dodgers!" bawled the sheriff. "I'll have some, too. And if somebody's got a flask on his hip, spike mine with a good slug of red-eye."

He sat down beside Hatfield and rolled himself a cigarette. "I sent Hipless with half a dozen boys to drop a loop on the Circle P bunch as you told me to," he announced.

"Good," said Hatfield. "Hilton is the weak sister of that outfit. I think he'll talk to save his own neck. You should be able to get enough on 'em to put 'em away for a spell, at least. Send old Hang Soon over to the Bowtie. Garrett will give him a job. He's one hell of a good cook and he wasn't in on anything. Got another cigarette handy? I want to take it easy with this arm for a bit."

The sheriff proceeded to roll one. Hatfield accepted it and drew in a deep and satisfying lungful of smoke.

"It was a puzzler, all right," he remarked. "One of the worst I ever ran up against. First I'd suspect Preston, then I'd suspect Cartina. Then I'd suspect they were working together. Then I wouldn't know who or what to suspect with

Pierce Kimble weaving in and out of the picture like a black cat dancing through moonfire to help tangle the twine. Preston gave me a nice lead when he tried to drygulch me that day on the trail. It was too darn obvious. Wilkes had been riding right alongside me all the time. But when we were heading up that slope, all of a sudden he scooted ahead and the hellion cracked down with his rifle from the crest. It was perfectly plain that it was Wilkes' chore to lead me into the ambush. But Wilkes was killed and I wasn't. It left me up in the air for quite a while until I tumbled to the truth. Preston callously sacrificed Wilkes to make the thing look good."

"It would have," agreed the sheriff. "Nobody would have suspected him with one of his own men found drygulched along with you. He was a snake-blooded hellion for fair."

"He was all of that," Hatfield nodded, "with a cold, keen brain. When he saw he'd failed, because of his defective rifle, he hightailed it, contacted a couple of his devilish Riders and laid another trap for me in his bunkhouse. And when he rode in with his bunch after pulling the payroll robbery and saw he'd failed again, he never turned a hair. He thought fast and managed to get rid of me without suspecting a thing. I just sort of absently noted that the rigs were equipped with saddle pouches, an out of the ordinary thing, and that the pouches were plumped out with something. But the meaning of it didn't dawn on me until later. So I got to town, heard about the robbery over the other side of the desert, and here come Fernando Cartina and Pierce Kimble nicely powdered with desert dust. Then Cartina proceeded to lie about where he was that night."

"What was he doing out on the desert?" asked the sheriff.

"Hunting for that ornery half-brother of his, Pierce Kimble," Hatfield replied. "Cartina tried to tell himself that Kimble was going straight, but just the same he wasn't sure. When he heard of the robbery and realized that Kimble had been away from the spread all afternoon and evening, he hustled out to hunt for him and provide him with an alibi if he happened to need one. Mistaken loyalty, that's all. Kimble had been in on the robbery, of course. He was working with Preston all the time. I don't know for sure, but I strongly suspect that Preston was one of the Graham gang when he was in Arizona. There were quite a few apparently respectable ranchers mixed up with that outfit. Anyhow, he knew Kimble in Arizona when he was Bill Graham and they got together again over here. That's how Preston was able to get all the inside information he needed. Kimble handled most of the details of Cartina's business which includes mine, cattle and banking tie-ups. He knew when stuff was to be moved, where, and how. It was a perfect set-up and continually reflected on Cartina. In fact, I was never perfectly sure about Cartina until after Kimble died. You'll remember commenting on the fact that after

Kimble died, the robberies and hold-ups abruptly stopped. Naturally Preston's source of inside information was dried up. He could only make a try for something everybody knew about, like the bullion shipment."

He paused a moment, chuckling. "That busted rifle pin was another tangler. Down in Mexico, when I grabbed his rifle after he came close to shooting Garrett, I found it had a brand-new firing pin. Fine! But when I got a chance to look at Cartina's rife in his ranchhouse, I'm darned if I didn't find he had a nice new one, too. Coincidence, that's all, firing-pins often get busted, but it helped to confuse matters. Checking with the gunsmith, however, I learned that Cartina had brought his rife in himself to be fixed, which he would hardly have done if he'd had anything to cover up. And anyway, while he's a darn nice jigger and I like him, by that time I'd pretty definitely decided that he wasn't hefty enough on the brain side to be running such an outfit as was operating in this section."

"It's a wonder to me that Preston didn't do for you when he had you down in Mexico," the sheriff grunted.

"Perhaps he would have if I hadn't stuck to him like a leech," Hatfield replied. "Preston knew very well that if I died, he'd die too, and that wasn't exactly convenient for him at the moment. I've a notion, though, that it pleased him to play the game that way. He wanted to rescue Tom Garrett. Lonnie had promised to marry him if he did. He wanted Lonnie and the Bowtie, the most valuable piece of property in the section, and by marrying her he'd have gotten both. Preston looked ahead and wanted a backlog in case his plans failed. But it was down there that I really decided he was *El Hombre* and in cahoots with Cheno. Everything worked out too nicely. Cheno's *soldados* chased us for quite a ways, but they took good care never to catch up. No better riders in the world than those *vaqueros*, and they were well mounted. Tom Garrett was forking a crowbait that slowed us up. Just the same, they kept their distance and the shooting they did was over our heads. So Preston came back to Texas a hero and was in solid with Garrett's friends and everybody else. He figured he'd tangled my twine for me again, which he had. But it was the beginning of the end for him. After that I was after him and nobody else. Of course he'd been after me ever since Kimble recognized me for a Ranger."

"And you settled down right in the middle of the nest of snakes," the sheriff marvelled.

"Safest place I could pick," said Hatfield. "They didn't dare to do away with me in a fashion that would direct suspicion toward them. Then Captain Bill would have had a troop stationed down here, and that's just what they didn't want. But having me with them all the time cramped their style. That's why they never interfered with me and allowed me to run around loose. They were glad to get me out of the way."

"Really think Preston planned to take over Mexico?" asked the sheriff.

"Hard to tell," Hatfield admitted. "Perhaps he just aimed for the rich pickings that would come his way in the course of a row like that along the Border. Cheno was his front, of course. If Cheno had succeeded in overthrowing Diaz, the chances are Preston would have moved in and taken over. After all, he was half Spanish and the notion may have appealed to him. Anyhow, he figured he had everything to win and nothing to lose. If the uprising failed it would be Cheno who would face the firing squad with his back to a wall, just as Maximilian did. Preston would have slid from under. He was mighty shrewd and hard to pin anything onto. So finally I gave up trying and concentrated on finding his hideaway up here. The *peons* he had hogtied through terror were his weak link. I felt sure that sooner or later I'd get one to talk, and that's just what happened. Well, guess I'll ride over to the Bowtie for the rest of the night and tomorrow. Got a little something to attend to over there before I head back to the Post and another chore."

"Good huntin'!" chuckled the sheriff. Hatfield grinned and said nothing, but there was a look of pleasant anticipation in his green eyes.

The sheriff chuckled again. "Beats all," he said. "One Ranger, single-handed, busts up a revolution!"

"Well," smiled Hatfield, "there was just one revolution!"